VENUS TRAP

MAYA DANIELS

Vinci Books

vinci-books.com

Published by Vinci Books Ltd in 2026

1

Copyright © Maya Daniels 2019

The author has asserted their moral right to be identified as the author of this work in accordance with the Copyright, Designs and Patents Act 1988. This work is a work of fiction. Names, characters, places and incidents are the product of the author's imagination or are used fictitiously. Any resemblance to actual persons, living or dead, places and incidents is entirely coincidental.
All rights reserved. No part of this publication may be copied, reproduced, distributed, stored in any retrieval system, or transmitted in any form or by any means, including photocopying, recording, or other electronic or mechanical methods, nor used as a source for any form of machine learning including AI datasets, without the prior written permission of the publisher.
The publisher and the author have made every effort to obtain permissions for any third party material used in this book and to comply with copyright law. Any queries in this respect should be brought to the attention of the publisher and any omissions will be corrected in future editions.
A CIP catalogue record for this book is available from the British Library.
Paperback ISBN: 9781036705893
The EU GPSR authorised representative is Logos Europe, 9 rue Nicolas Poussion, 17000 La Rochelle, France contact@logoseurope.eu

By Maya Daniels

Hidden Portals Trilogy
Venus Trap
The First Secret

Chronicles of Forbidden Witchery
Resting Witch Face
Pitch a Witch
Witch Please
Payback is a Witch

The Necronomicon Guardian
The Magician
The High Priestess

The Broken Halos Series
The Devil is in the Details
Speak of the Devil
Encounter with the Devil
The Devil in Disguise
To Look the Devil in the Eye
Better The Devil You Know
Give a Devil His Due

The Last Note Series
Sound

Sonata

Daywalker Series
Investigated
Infiltrated
Instigated
Initiated
Infuriated
Ignited

Infernal Regions for the Unprepared
Black Hand
Lower World
Everlasting Fire
Place of Torment
Hellfire To Come

The Courtless Fae Series
Secret Origins

New Blood Rising
Rebirth - Risorgimento
Overthrown - Rovesciamento
Recognition - Riconoscimento

The Gatekeepers Legacy
Legacy of Water
Legacy of Fire
Legacy of Spirit

Honor Among Thieves

Stolen Magic

Stolen Oath

By Maya Daniels

The Cursed Kingdom

Chapter One

A storm was raging and the night was as dark as a black hole that's trying to suck in everything around it. The skies seemed like a portal to Hell as lightning strikes split the dark gray clouds open and thunder echoed, making the ground shake with its force. Winds tore through the trees, almost bending them in half while branches were breaking off and flying through the air. No living thing stirred in the woods. No one dared to venture outside of their shelters while predators and prey huddled together; the instinct to survive stronger than the desire to hunt or run. Each lightning strike, spreading through the sky like a cobweb, was the only thing making it visible enough for the man braving the storm to continue walking. Even with his enhanced vision, it would've been impossible to see a finger in front of his face in the all-consuming darkness. Just when he thought things couldn't get worse, the skies opened and icy rain poured down on him like from a faucet. The next lightning strike illuminated his angelic face, where displeasure was clearly written but determination burned hot in his eyes. It looked like even the weather was doing its best to stop him from continuing on. He had been summoned by his king for a reason. Besides, nothing was as dangerous as him in these woods.

His hair made rivulets of rain run down his neck and inside his shirt. Closing his eyes, he lifted his face towards the skies and spread his arms wide as if daring the weather to do its worst. The knee length coat flapped in the strong winds around him, but he stood firm as if laughing in the face of the gods. This was only bad timing on his part, not a bad omen. Most definitely not the worst day of his life, either. His immortal life, that is. The one he didn't ask for but received nonetheless.

Lowering his arms slowly, he gripped the closest tree next to him and pushed himself forwards. Refusing to let thoughts of his long-gone mortal life penetrate the calm and accepting façade he'd spent centuries creating, he continued along the path. Where he was going, it was best to stay as cold and as emotionless as he could be, because if they can't find a weakness, they can't exploit it. Only the strong and the cunning survive, and he has been around for centuries. He almost believed himself that there was no sentimentality left in him, just calculating logic.

A branch as wide as his torso slammed next to him and only his fast reflexes saved him from being impaled where he stood. The haunting sounds of the whistling winds amplified as his senses went on full alert. Standing unnaturally still, he tried his best to hear beyond the wind, albeit unsuccessfully. A prickling sensation alerted him that he was being watched, but for the first time, he couldn't tell by whom. He couldn't even say what it was that had the eyes trained on his movement.

At the last moment, he distinguished the sound coming

from his right, but he wasn't fast enough. He wasn't dead, thankfully, but he was hurt. Excruciating pain tore through his arm, and he found himself unable to move. Lightning fast, he grabbed hold of the arrow pinning his arm to the tree and pulled it off while sliding around the tree trunk to hide from view.

"The predator becoming a prey." He chuckled under his breath while the uneasy feeling kept growing in his stomach.

"How does it feel?" a woman's voice softly purred in his ear, making the hairs on his neck stand on end.

Jerking his head in the direction he heard the voice coming from, he saw no one. How he was able to hear the whispered words so clearly above the winds and the storm was beyond him. It was almost as if they were in his mind. Unwilling to be a sitting duck, he stood and bolted through the trees as fast as his unnatural speed would allow him. His coat, wet and flapping behind him, catching on branches and shrubs while altering his speed, did not stop him. It might seem cowardly to some, but if you want to live and fight another day, sometimes running was the smart plan of action. Only a fool will stay against uneven odds, and a fool he was not. Grateful that none of his people would witness this moment, he concentrated all his efforts on getting out of there as soon as possible. Still holding onto the arrow, he streaked through the trees, moving left or right at the last moment so he wouldn't collide with them. Where he was headed should not be that far now.

As his speed was increasing, so was the storm getting stronger. With his mind firmly set on escaping whatever it is that was hunting him, he never noticed the dark figure following just above his head. The buzzing sound of the wings was covered by the monstrous thunders that were shaking the woods. Nor did he hear her gleeful chuckle at his fear.

"Run, little rabbit, run," she whispered for his ears only, making him stumble before tripping on dried roots and sprawling on the forest floor, taking few trees down with him. She laughed out loud when his body bounced off of the ancient tree that stopped his rolling. His immortal essence was calling to her nature like a beacon, begging to be consumed.

Stopping not far from where he landed, she watched him unsuccessfully try to lift himself up. After a couple of tries, he finally shook his head and raised himself to his knees. Blood was still running down his arm where she had pierced him with her arrow. The angelic face was gone, and in its place, an angry vampire stood. With fangs descended and eyes glowing with an amber hue, he searched the darkness while water ran down his face, making him finally look like the predator he said he was. Not that it would help him, but he didn't know that. They have been tamed, becoming complacent amongst the humans with no one stronger than them. They thought they were on top of the food chain. This little vampire will learn something different tonight. Too bad he won't live long enough to tell the story. He was the fourth in a row to meet an unfortunate end, and she covered her tracks perfectly. Not that she cared, but it was better for now.

She knew she shouldn't come here. It was not the time, but curiosity has always been stronger than reason. She wanted to see for herself the place that had banished her kind to live. To barely survive while being secluded and hidden, when the humans killed their Queen. The cursed humans have shunned the Fae, but embraced the bloodsuckers. The time to pay will come soon enough, only not today. The humans will not pay today, but the vampire in front of her would. Passing above his head, she gripped the branches of the tree tightly with her thighs. He was still looking around, searching and feeling almost confident with his back towards the tree that no one can sneak up on him. Lowering her upper body, her head was now hanging right on top of his. With a smile, she reached for her arrow, raising it up. "Up here, handsome," she purred, and his head snapped up.

Her smile grew as his eyes, locked on hers, widened in horror before she slammed her arrow through his skull. The thunder covered his scream before it was abruptly cut off. Pulling her arrow free and dropping to the ground in front of his body, she wiped it off on his clothing before placing it back in her quiver. Her body transformed back to its human-like appearance as it touched the forest floor.

"Well, that was uneventful," she mused to herself, looking around. "I thought you'd put up more of a fight. I can see now that Lazarus was right. This will be like younglings' play if all of you are the same."

Closing her eyes, she pulled on his essence and consumed it, the shimmering glow lost in the flashes of the storm. A shiver ran down her spine; this one was as powerful as each of the other three before him.

With one last lingering look at the dead vampire, she smoothed the water out of her hair and started slowly walking back. They might see she was missing, and there would be hell to pay if Lazarus found out where she was. Even that wouldn't stop her from coming into this realm. Nothing can stop her once she sets her mind to it. Lazarus should be forever grateful she is duty-bound and that what he wants aligns with her desire for revenge. If that were not the case, she was sure only one of them would be left standing. For now, playing obedient solder was working for her. She wasn't sure how much longer she could play the submissive and allow him to strut around, treating her like she was below him. The Dark Fae king had no idea what he was dealing with, but for everyone's sake, she was hoping things would get settled soon. That hope was the only thing stopping her from unleashing her wrath on everyone and everything around her. With one last look over her shoulder, she disappeared between two ancient trees like she had never been there in the first place.

Chapter Two

"What was all the rush to get me here, Claude?" Raphael's words stopped everyone in their tracks as he walked into the large reception area.

The large open space had tall black pillar candles with flames flickering, reaching up towards the high ceiling. In their glow, the decorative golden crown moldings were casting shadows on the walls that danced around with each movement of the flames. Thick blood-red curtains were pulled tight over the floor-to-ceiling windows, hiding those inside from prying eyes. An elaborate dangling chandelier made entirely of crystal hung like a pendulum in the center, creating sparkling rainbows of colors with every beat of the music that was humming in the background. It was making Raphael dizzy when he looked at the faces around him. The marble tiles, shiny as mirrors, clicked under his feet as he made his way towards the raised platform on the other end.

Dozens of their kind were milling around, dressed in sheer clothing, leather and chains, holding their champagne flutes and pretending they were discussing something of great importance instead of gossiping like old ladies. Raphael knew better. All of them were there in the hope Claude would decide to share a bit of his blood, make a mistake to show weakness or choose to share his bed with one of them. That's all everyone ever wanted. Power or sex. It was pathetic to watch how intelligent beings turned into pathetic little worms. The silence was deafening as they parted in front of him like the Red Sea while his power crackled around him and the closest ones shivered or moaned. The lust in their in their eyes as they followed his progress like a rare piece of steak didn't go unnoticed. They would crawl on their hands and knees and bark like dogs if he so desired. The thought made the side of his mouth quirk a bit at the corner, but he kept his face expressionless. It was amusing but not worth his time or effort. Lately, nothing was. Raphael's eyes didn't leave the man sitting sprawled in a high chair elevated above the rest, his tuxedo rumpled albeit immaculate at first glance.

"Ah! Raphael, my friend! I see you finally made it...after I sent the third messenger to bring you here." Claude's smile and easygoing demeanor contradicted the angry glint in his grey eyes.

"You do know it's the 21st century, no? Humans invented cell phones for that reason alone, so they don't need to send messengers." Reaching the platform where Claude was perched on his chair, Raphael slowly placed his hands in the pockets of his pants, flicking his suit jacket back and looking around at the gawkers. "Don't the rest of you have something better to do? Get the hell out of here, and I don't want to see any of you until I leave."

Although his words were conversational and soft, they were like a whip to the rest of the crowd. In less than half a minute the large room was empty, leaving him and Claude alone.

"You're not here one minute and you're already killing all my fun. I see nothing has changed since the last time I saw you," Claude drawls, narrowing his eyes at Raphael "How long has it been? A decade? Two?"

Not long enough, Raphael thought to himself but didn't voice it. They have been friends for centuries, but Claude could be a bit too much most of the time and reminded Raphael of days he would rather forget. From the day Raphael was turned, Claude had been the only one bringing him back from the brink when their maker would do anything to drive Raphael crazy and feral. It was Anissa's mission, like she was feeding off his sanity instead of his blood, ever since she saw him that cursed night when he was still human. His life had been worse than hell until he had his chance to change that. Pain gripped Raphael's chest and bile rose in his throat, so he pushed it away. Some things were better left unspoken.

The silence stretched between them as he really looked at his friend. Claude's dark hair was not in his usual slick ponytail but seemed like he had just moved it out of his face without brushing it. The grey eyes that always had a calculating look in them were now missing the sparkle and they look muted somehow. Barely visible dark circles lined his eyes, and as Raphael paid closer attention, he realized there was makeup on Claude's face. The shock of seeing that made him take a step back as if someone had punched him in the face.

"What in the world is going on? And what the fuck happened to you?" Worry made Raphael's deep voice boomed like a cannon in the empty hall, making Claude wince at the volume of it.

"Keep your voice down or I will silence you for eternity!" Claude hissed through clenched teeth, reminding Raphael that although this was his friend, he was the vampire king, after all. He had enough power to back up his words, feeding off of the rest of their species. Raphael gave up that right when he helped him take the throne. Maybe Claude didn't have enough power to threaten Raphael, but he didn't want to be king or deal with everyone either. So, showing respect even when Claude was being obnoxious was a small price to pay and he did it willingly.

"I apologize, my king. It was a friend being worried for a friend. Not meant as an insult." Almost inconceivably, Raphael lowered his head in a show of respect, being loud enough to be heard by those snooping around.

He couldn't bring himself to play an obedient fool. He had enough power on his own that if it came down between him or Claude, he wasn't sure that his king would be the last one standing, despite all the extra power coursing through him.

"I know...I know." With a sigh, Claude lifted himself from the chair, and walking past Raphael, he gestured with his fingers to be followed. Without another word, Raphael was right on his heels; curiosity and worry riding him hard. What could possibly worry the arrogant Claude this much?

Walking the hallways of the mansion felt strange to him after all the years Raphael had done his best to stay away from it. With each year, he withdrew more and more until there was nothing that could bring him outside of his own home. His books were his salvation; otherwise he might just meet the sun and end it all. Every time he was around his own kind, the memories of things he had done, or were done to him, would start haunting him and he couldn't deal with that. So he stayed away. After centuries, the years started weighing heavily on his shoulders, and he often wondered if living this hollow existence was worth it. Looking around, he still couldn't find any pleasure in the priceless pieces of art hanging on the walls or all the expensive decor that if sold, could feed a village for a year. With no prospect of finding a mate, they all wondered aimlessly through the centuries, looking for things that were lost to them forever. Their maker parted with her immortal life, taking with her all the secrets she held dear to her heart. That was how she held them all by the leash, how she manipulated them to do what she asked, by making promises of a future that she took from them when she made them creatures of the night. Now, with all hopes for a mate gone that he was responsible for, the rest of his kind played politics and fought for power. Raphael's cold heart sent a pang of longing through him and he clenched his teeth. He would not let those thoughts insert themselves in his mind. Not now, not ever!

A rustling of clothing and light footsteps could be heard, but they didn't see anyone on their way to Claude's office. Like cockroaches, the rest of the residents scurry around making Raphael sick to the stomach of how low they have fallen. How low his actions long time ago made them come, by being selfish and acting out of pain and anger. With clenched fists, he followed his friend, and looking at Claude's stiff shoulders, got his mind back on the present problem. As they finally reached the double doors of the only room in the mansion that was soundproofed for their enhanced hearing, Raphael's feet moved faster, as though he could escape his thoughts by giving himself something else to worry about. But they would come back, like leeches they will suck him dry, emerging from the murky ponds of his mind where he has pushed them to haunt him for as long as he lives. *Not today!* he declared to himself with conviction.

"What's going on?" The door was barely closed before he turned on his friend ready to bite out of frustration.

"Take a seat." Pointing at the leather sofa, Claude walked to the bar in the corner, where he filled up a glass of scotch mixed with vampire blood.

Humans still believed stupid stories that vampires lurked in the night searching to find one of them and suck them dry – or – that they were not real. It was laughable to hear, but it allowed them to live by themselves without having to deal with paranoia or righteous assholes wanting to play heroes. Life would've been much easier if they could feed on humans, but they couldn't. They needed the blood of an immortal to survive. So they manipulated, tricked and even abused and killed their own to keep breathing. Raphael knew this first-hand. Acid burned his throat and he pushed those thought away, as well. This was why he stayed away and hated being amongst his kind. Those fucking memories and thoughts that would make him want to end it once and for all.

Reluctantly Raphael perched on the edge of the sofa, unable to sit and relax but unwilling to anger Claude more than he already had. Shaking his head at the bottle Claude was pointing his way, he tried to stay calm. The longer his king stayed quiet, the worse the news was going to be. He knew it as well as he knew his own name. Gulping down one glass, Claude refilled it again before coming to sit opposite Raphael.

"Philip is dead."

Everything around Raphael stopped like he'd been

suspended in time and space. Claude's words echoed in his head on repeat, and he found himself unable to even blink.

"Did you hear me?" Anger colored Claude's words as he leaned towards Rafael from his end of the sofa, glaring.

"He's dead." Raphael's words sounded hollow, even to himself. He tried to remember when was the last time he had seen or even heard from his friends. The six of them made a pact long time ago to not stand in each other's way when Raphael decided he had had enough and was taking control over his life and his sanity. In his solitude, Raphael had lost contact with all of them.

"Yes," Claude nodded his head a few times as if satisfied that he was heard. "Also Valeria, Boris and Darian. All of them are dead."

"This is not a time to play games, Claude. If you have killed them, you and I, we have a big problem!" Jumping from his perch on the sofa, Raphael loomed over Claude while clenching his fists so he didn't grab the fucker by his neck and strangle him.

"Why would I kill them? We had a pact, we were all sticking to it! Do I look like a fool to you?" Standing up as well, Claude faced Raphael with as angry an expression as ever.

"Who was it?" The words were barely a whisper, but there was no mistaking the promise of death in Raphael's voice.

"If I told you, you wouldn't believe me." Lifting a hand to stop Raphael's argument, Claude walked over towards his desk. "But I"m going to show you anyway. I couldn't find any clue about who was behind it until now. I'm still trying to get over the shock myself."

Walking over to the wall, Claude moved the painting

and started unlocking the safe behind it. Raphael found himself unable to move, so only his eyes tracked Claude's movements. After rummaging through it, Claude slowly turned around, gingerly holding something in both hands as though it were some ceremonial athame. At first, Raphael couldn't comprehend what it was that he was looking at. Then he realized what it was, his brain was just in denial.

"Is that..." his words trailed off.

"We found it in Philip's hand. When he didn't show up last night, I sent out a search party since I knew he was on his way. We found him in the woods not far from here." Claude jerked his hands in Raphael's direction as if asking him to take the object.

"That's impossible!" Raphael shook his head as if trying to clear it.

"Oh, it is possible, I assure you. And they're picking us off like ripe cherries, one by one!"

Slowly lifting his hand, Raphael's fingers wrapped around the arrow in Claude's hands. Taking hold of it, he brought it closer to his face, unable to stop himself from admiring the intricate designs on it that still had a faint glow. A mild shock passed to his hand from it, giving him goosebumps from head to toe. With an astonished look, he tried to comprehend that what he held in his hand was an object out of fairytales, a myth, as far as he knew. His fist tightened around it as he swallowed hard, thinking about what his friends might have been feeling in those last moments. Now he only had one friend left in this world. All the others were dead while he hid between four walls wallowing in his misery. Humans would sell their souls for immortality while he despised it. His chest tightened with a mixture of grief and anger.

"The Dark Fae are back, after so many centuries. I've

only heard stories about this." The words barely pass his barely-moving lips as his eyes lifted from the arrow and locked with Claude's. "The Wild Hunt is coming…" The pregnant silence stretched between them as they stood there, considering the implications this brought with it.

Chapter Three

The insistent knocking on the door made Artemis groan and bury her head in her pillow. If whoever was standing at her door didn't walk away soon, they'd regret it. She wasn't a grumpy person, just exhausted. Passing through the portal to the human realm undetected took its toll on her because she had to do it in her shifted form. Four nights in a row she went back and forth with no one wiser about her exploration. *Well, no one but the dead bloodsuckers, but they can't tell now, can they?* her mind supplied as her ego chuckled. That was how she decided that to call her visits 'explorations.' If she just happened to find a wandering vampire, unintentionally, of course, it was to no fault of her own. She was just clearing the path sooner than expected, that was all. Just as her body relaxed again with the silence, her door banged open, making her jump from the bed in one motion.

"Oh, you're awake!" Fern roamed his crystal-blue eyes over her naked body, making her want to slap him in the face.

"You have exactly one blink of an eye to tell me why

you're in my room before I separate your head from your body." Undisturbed by her nakedness, Artemis placed her hands on her hips.

Fern has been trying for a very long time to get into her bed, so it came as no surprise that it took him long moments of looking at her with hungry eyes before he answered. He was a very handsome male, with his black hair falling straight over his broad shoulders and his blue eyes standing out stark against his caramel complexion. Many of the others would've jumped at the opportunity to have his perfect body tangled with theirs, but not Artemis. Her nature didn't allow her to do what the rest of them did. It was in who she was as Fae that a male would have to physically prove he was stronger or more cunning then her before she would let him inside her body. Even if she liked him, and she did find Fern pleasing to the eye, unless he proved he was stronger than her, there will be nothing between them. Not even for the night. It made for a lonely existence, but she couldn't go against her nature.

"The king wants to see you." Fern didn't even had a decency to look at her eyes while talking to her; he was too busy trying not to let his eyes linger on parts of her body. "He didn't look very pleased when he sent me to get you."

Keeping her face expressionless while her mind started whirling with all the reasons Lazarus could find to be displeased with her, Artemis moved around the room, picking her clothes up. She'd dropped them haphazardly on the floor when she got back the night before, not caring about anything but her bed.

"Did he say why?" Shoving her legs into her pants, she wiggled her hips to pull the tight fabric up. A smirk pulled at her lips when Fern's eyes stayed glued to her hips while he shook his head to indicate he had no idea.

"Let's go then. Lead the way." Pulling the boots on to her feet, she snatched the corset and started walking out.

"Wait!" Fern grabbed her shoulder, and before he could blink, his back hit the floor hard and Artemis was kneeling on his chest, snarling at him.

"Don't touch me, Fern! I have told you that, many times. Next time you do it will be your last!"

"I didn't mean anything by it." Fern groaned, yet his eyes kept flicking from her face to her breasts. "There are so many of my kind milling outside in the halls and the tension is almost palpable in the air. Something is going on, I just don't know what yet. I didn't think you'll want to be anything but battle-ready when you walk out."

"You know that would've sounded more convincing if you could look me in the eyes, right?" Pushing off of his chest and making him groan louder, Artemis got to her feet.

Pulling the corset over her chest, she pulled her long violet hair into a ponytail as she walked through her door. She could hear Fern's footsteps behind her as he caught up with her. Keeping her head straight and not looking at anyone else, she headed right for the king's office. As she was about to take a left turn towards it, Fern stopped her in her tracks.

"He's in the formal reception hall." At his words, Artemis looked at him over her shoulder, her violet eyes sparkling with anger. There was no mistaking the worry in his voice. "He asked for you to see him there." Fern finished by indicating with his arm that she should descend the winding stairway to the ground floor of the palace.

Turning around, she walked with head held high and squared shoulders, her hips swaying seductively. She could feel their eyes on her, their whispers behind her back, but she ignored them all. Artemis concentrated on staying calm so she could deal with Lazarus. He knew how to push her buttons and get a reaction better than anyone else she knew. Her hand twitched from the desire to have her bow in it, but it would be considered an insult to Lazarus to show up armed when she was summoned. Clenching her fist at her side, she entered the formal hall and was very proud of herself for not breaking her stride or flinching when she saw what waited for her there.

Lazarus was sitting on his throne in all his half-naked glory. Loose black pants made of the finest silk were covering his lower body, while his chest was bare and his black wings were spread on either side behind him. Unnervingly, his emerald eyes were tracking her every movement as though he'd known the exact moment she would walk through the doors. His beautiful face was expressionless, giving him an almost statue-like appearance. There were others present, but Artemis was a hunter. She knew who the biggest threat was, and all of her focus was on him. She ignored everyone else, at least for the moment.

"You sent for me." Dropping on one knee as she reached the throne, Artemis bowed her head slightly "...my king," she added as an afterthought.

"No need to bow to me, my daughter. Stand up!" Lazarus's deep voice sounded kind and oh, so very fake. "You disobey my orders but bow to me." His look was so intent that Artemis had no doubt that if he could, he would have burned her to ashes with his eyes.

"I haven't disobeyed anything." Standing up, she lifted her chin defiantly at him.

"I see." Nodding, Lazarus turned his head slightly to look at Fern over her shoulder. Artemis's heart jumped to her throat and dropped to her feet in the same moment. "Did you bring what I asked?"

She watched Fern brush past her as he walked up to the throne and handed her bow and arrows to Lazarus. How she hadn't seen him carrying it was beyond her. A frown pulled at her face when she saw it. Her weapon was connected to her, it was part of her. What in the worlds were they planning to do with it? Fern walked back to stand one step behind her, but not before sending her an apologetic glance that she responded to with a glare. She would deal with him later.

"Is this not your weapon, my daughter?" His words were irritating her, especially his constant repetition of 'my daughter' as if it needed confirmation every two seconds.

"It is." She didn't blink or break eye contact, so she didn't miss the barely-visible lift of his mouth. Anxiety almost drilled a hole in her stomach, and she wanted to scream at him but stood still.

"And you have an arrow missing? An arrow that can ruin all of our plans if it's found!"

He said it conversationally, but all the color drained from Artemis's face. Without thinking, she rushed up to his throne and snatched the arrows from his hands, rummaging through them. Lazarus didn't say a word, just watching her. Sure as hell, one arrow was missing. Whoever found it could summon her now at their whim, since the weapon was tied to her essence. Her eyes darting left and right while her mind worked hard to remember where it could be, she ignored Lazarus, who stared at her, unblinking. After a second, she remembered piercing the vampire with an arrow before killing him with another. More importantly, how on earth did he know that her arrow was missing when she was so sure that no one knew about her sneaking through the portal? Pressure was building in her temples to the point that she felt her head was about to explode. At the moment she knew she needed to act calm, as if it were an everyday occurrence for an arrow attached to her soul to go missing. She could worry about the rest later, away from his inspection. Her eyes flicked to her father.

"I will get it back. I know where it is," she told him, trying her best to act calm.

"And where is that?" His eyebrows lifted halfway up his forehead while his face remained the picture of innocence.

"In the human realm," Artemis answered, having no other choice, and the gasps around her made her fume with anger.

"You will get your arrow, and when you return, you will receive your punishment for disobeying my orders." Malice glinted in Lazarus's eyes as he threw the bow at her, dismissing her.

"Yes, my king." Grabbing hold of her weapon, Artemis lifted her head up and walked out of the hall the same way she had entered. She'd be damned if she showed anything but indifference to everyone here. She would retrieve her arrow and accept her punishment. It wasn't like it would be the first time she was punished.

Chapter Four

Inside Claude's mansion, things were becoming increasingly heated up by the moment. Those that stayed there with him felt the tension escalating while Claude pretended that everything was normal and Raphael locked himself in the library. Whispers and pointed glances were sent Claude's way as he sat nonchalantly on his chair surveying the crowd. He could feel their unease as well as their calculating glances making him smirk internally while maintaining his expressionless mask. They might think it was a perfect opportunity to challenge him, but if one of them decided to try his luck, it might do Claude some good, giving him the opportunity to take out all his frustration and anxiety on the unlucky one.

The longer Raphael stayed silent behind closed doors, the more the idea of a fight appealed to Claude. He knew that if anyone could find a way to put an end to this mess, it would be Raphael. The man was a walking library on his own and more powerful than Claude wanted to admit. While others of their kind collected riches and bought homes around the world, Raphael collected knowledge while investing in businesses that couldn't be linked to him. How he managed to keep only one house and not make the humans suspicious was beyond Claude, who had to admit to himself that he got pulled along with the rest of them when it came to living a life of luxury. He loved power and prestige. Without it, there wouldn't be any benefit to being an immortal since Anissa took all her secrets to the grave. While the rest of his friends were turned without a say, Claude had been the one who was seeking immortality when he heard the stories. Centuries later he never regretted his decision, but he was close to regretting it now. If what he suspected was coming, he might have bigger problems than merely keeping their kind hidden and staying at the top of their line.

A movement got his attention, pulling him out of his thoughts. A blonde bombshell was sauntering around, sending heated glances his way from under her lashes before she slowly lowered herself on a chair opposite him. Her dress covered nothing, the sheer fabric allowing her nipples to point at him and her sex to glisten in the muted light where she was seating, her legs slightly parted in invitation. Claude had seen her around but never paid much attention to her until now. As he looked at her, she took a leisurely sip from her glass, slowly licking the last drop from the rim, making his loins stir. Her brown eyes flashed with an amber hue for a second, making sure he saw her arousal. Standing up, he crooked his finger at her to follow him as he headed for his rooms. If he had to wait for Raphael, no one said he had to sit and dwell on things. At least he found a way to make the time pass faster. Before she even closed the door behind her, he was on her like the predator he was. Her dress was gone and his fangs were rooted in her throat. *A great way to pass the time indeed,* thought Claude.

Raphael, on the other hand, felt like slamming his head on the massive mahogany desk he was sitting at. It had been hours since he started going through all the records they had on the Fae and the Wild Hunt, with no success. All he'd found was some assumptions written decades ago. They sounded like a science fiction novel to him. A snort escaped him at the absurdity of anything sounding unrealistic to a vampire. Rubbing his hands over his face and through his hair, he unbuttoned the top few buttons of his shirt before taking his suit jacket off. Draping it on the chair, he walked to the shelves in hopes of finding another book with some relevant information. Leaning his shoulder on the bookshelf, he tried massaging his temples to elevate the pressure building in his head. It was very unfortunate that immortality did nothing to stop headaches.

As he was about to continue looking through the books, his eyes landed on a sleek silver box on one corner of the shelf. Frowning, he walked to it, and when he got near it, his eyes widened. Throwing back his head, he laughed out loud, his baritone echoing in the vast library.

"Well, what do you know! Claude, you sneaky little devil. Sending messengers like it's medieval Europe while a laptop is sitting forgotten in your house!" Still chuckling and shaking his head, he grabbed the laptop and walked back to the desk. Pushing everything aside, he opened it, turned it on, and as soon as he could, he started the search engine and started typing. If this didn't bring him closer to any firm information, nothing would.

After hours of reading through blogs, forums and ridiculous websites of people claiming to be fairies, he finally came across a site that got his attention—a coven open to all beliefs dedicated to worshiping the old gods. He had found many of those in his search, but this one nagged at him. There was something in the way they worded things that was raising red flags in his mind, giving him such a strong feeling of urgency that he felt compelled to go there. A shiver raked his frame and he decided it would be best for him to check it out. Looking at his watch, he realized that he had only a couple of hours left before sundown when he could go visit the address given on the site. It might be a bust, but at least he'd get out of the room before he went insane. He kept reading articles about the Fae, some making him shake his head, others making him frown with the ideas they painted in his head. There was no way the Fae could be that powerful. Formidable, without a doubt. More powerful than a vampire? He would have to see that to believe it.

Unprompted, his eyes locked on the arrow sitting at the corner of the desk. Maybe he already knew that they were more powerful, he just refused to admit it to himself. His fist clenched at the thought of never seeing his friends again. Unable to sit still any longer, he jumped off the chair, snatched his jacket and stormed out of the library. Between one moment and the next, he was standing in front of Claude's doors. Without thinking anything of it, he grabbed the door handles and pushed the doors open, walking inside.

"I think I found something..." Raphael's words trailed off as he froze a few steps inside the doorway.

A woman was bent over at the end of the bed with Claude looming over her. Both of them were naked, and it looked like Raphael had just walked in while they were having sex. Raphael's interruption made Claude turn to look his way, and that told an entirely different story. The woman's mouth was open not in pleasure but in pain as Claude drained the life out of her. He looked feral; his eyes blazed red and blood was splattered all over both of them and the bed. Raphael knew he needed to proceed carefully if he wished to avoid a fight with his friend.

"What happened, my king?" Raphael spoke softly, lifting his hands in submission so as not to startle Claude, who started snarling at him. "Did she not please you? I will find another for you. Let this one go." With each word, he took a barely visible step closer to the bed expecting Claude to attack him at any moment.

"Do not patronize me, Raphael!" Snarling the words, Claude snapped the woman's neck before grabbing her dress to wipe the blood off himself. "The bitch tried to kill me!" he spat, glaring at her twisted body.

At Claude's words, Raphael noticed all the bite wounds on his friend that looked like a wild animal had mauled him and he threw his head back laughing, unable to stop himself. Claude kept snarling about assholes and useless whores, but Raphael couldn't stop laughing. He didn't hear most of the words his friend said. After a while, Claude joined him, and they both ended up with tears in their eyes.

"Only you would laugh at something like this!" Claude gasped between chuckles, slapping a hand on his thigh.

"She did put up a good fight, my friend. It'll take a few days for all of that to heal." Shaking his head, Raphael grabbed a robe from the top of the dresser and handed it to Claude. "I'm going to check out a coven. In my search, it's the only thing that's given me a feeling that it can provide some answers. I'll be back as soon as I'm done. Keep everyone inside tonight. We don't need more deaths before we know for sure what we are dealing with."

"Should I go with you?" Claude wrapped the robe

around himself and started walking towards the bathroom. "Give me a moment to wash off the blood and we can leave."

"No need. I'll be back before you know it. I'm sure you'll need some time to make an example out of her. She'll wake up soon." Raphael pointed at the body that started twitching a little. A broken neck wouldn't kill them. So far, only ripping their heart out or exposing them to the sun could, but now, with this predicament they found themselves in, Fae weapons could too apparently. It just kept adding more shit to Raphael's plate and he was not happy about it at all.

"A coven, you say?" Stopping at the bathroom door and looking over his shoulder, Claude frowned at Raphael. "That's all we need, involving witches in this mess. If you're not back in a couple of hours, I'm coming after you."

"You almost sound sentimental, Claude. If you're not careful, I'll start believing you care." With a big grin on his face, Raphael turned and started walking out of the room. "I'll be back as fast as I can, mother!" he called over his shoulder and went on his way, chuckling at the obscenities Claude sent his way.

Chapter Five

"Artemis, wait!" Fern's voice echoed around her like a gong.

"I would stay away from me at the moment, Fern, if I were you." Not turning in his direction or slowing her steps, Artemis continued up the stairs towards her room.

"I know you're upset with me, but you must know I had no choice in the matter." As Fern reached her, he lifted a hand towards her shoulder, but at the last moment thought better of it and dropped it to his side "I just followed orders, the same way you do."

"There is always a choice. You just picked the one that suited you most." Watching him from the corner of her eye, Artemis didn't miss the grimace on his face. She'd hit the bullseye with that comment, and he knew it. "I don't need your apologies, so do me a favor and go back to wherever you're needed. I have nothing to say to you."

"You can stop the attitude!" he snarled "Everyone needs allies, and you're no exception. Don't push away those who might be useful when you need one," Fern hissed at her through clenched teeth.

"May the fates save me from allies like you." Stopping at the door of her room, she turned towards him. "I need no one but myself, Fern. If there is one thing I have absolute faith in, it's that I can always count on myself, as it should be. Even your shadow leaves you in the dark. Don't ever forget that."

She watched him hang his head in defeat, or maybe guilt, his hair falling over his shoulders and covering his face like a curtain. Artemis didn't feel guilty for calling him out on his misguided loyalties. Guilt was something associated with humans, from what she'd heard. She didn't have time for such sentimentalities. Self-preservation and anger, on the other hand, she knew very well. Giving Fern one more look, she leaned against the door. Opening it behind her back, she stepped through it just as he lifted his head and took a breath, looking like he was trying to say something. With an arrogant twitch of her lips, she closed the door in his face.

Pressing her palms and forehead on the door, Artemis closed her eyes. She had no room in her life for impulsiveness and curiosity at this time. What possessed her to go to the human realm, not once but four times? Moreover, to kill each time she was there, too. Something was changing in the human realm, and she felt herself growing stronger with each passing moment. She'd intended to see if she could find out where these changes were coming from when she decided to go through the portal, but she saw the first vampire that night. Her instincts kicked in and he didn't help much, with the way he acted. She might have let him live, and maybe it wouldn't have come to this if he hadn't mistaken her for a human. A snort escaped her as she remembered that first night. Only a fool would mistake her for a human with her dark violet hair swinging like a thick rope on her back down to her hips, and her violet eyes giving off a glow that was unmistakably Fae.

That thought stopped her, making her lift her head and open her eyes. Could it be? Could they honestly not know how a Fae should look? It had been centuries since any of her kind hastepped set foot in the human realm—through no fault of their own, of course. Last time a Fae had seen was the day of the Great War, when humans thought hunting Fae was some kind of sport and they would get immortality as a reward. That had been the day her mother had stood against them to protect her people. It was the day she died, cut down by humans and vampires who had banded together. The vampires feasted on her blood like animals as the humans watched and stripped her of all her jewels and adornments with their greedy little hands while she breathed her last breath. A sharp, crippling pain pierced Artemis's chest, and she pressed her hands to its center.

Artemis was just a youngling at the time, but she's heard the stories. As she was growing up, Lazarus spent an unmeasurable amount of time telling her stories about her mother, too. How beautiful and brave she was. Strong and so determined to protect her people that she refused to hide. Artemis remembered all the stories, word for word, to this day. That was why when Lazarus asked, she immediately agreed to join the Wild Hunt. She worked hard and relentlessly for a long time, but now she was leading it. Artemis was in charge, and she would be the first and last face the humans and vampires would see when the portal fully opened. That thought made her straighten up, pushing the memories deep down. She needed to get her arrow and return to accept her punishment. Artemis knew it would be something severe, and she didn't want to prolong the time before it was applied. The longer she waited, more time it would take for her to heal.

Walking up to the wall where all her weapons were displayed, her fingers trailed over the daggers, swords and knives glinting in the sunlight coming through the arched windows. Their intricate designs and jeweled handles looked like a sky full of colorful stars on the stone wall. She wasn't sure why, but she had a feeling it would be better to bring a variety of weapons rather than relying on only her bow. By now, probably half the realm knew where she was going. Artemis wouldn't put it past them to try something stupid. It'd be a shame if she had to kill her own, but kill them she would if they tried to get in her way. The soft knock at the door came just as she hid the fifth knife in one of the many hidden holsters of her corset and boots.

"I thought I was clear when I told you I have nothing more..." Her words trailed off as Artemis yanked the door open and saw it wasn't Fern standing there. "Ivy? What can I do for you?" The beautiful blonde dreamweaver standing at her door could put the sun to shame with her glowing skin, silver eyes and shining golden hair. Her gifts were as beautiful as her physical appearance—being able to heal anyone while they slept, or make sure they never woke up. Many envied her for that, and Ivy loved every second of it.

"I can't come by simply to check on you?" Ivy's thin eyebrow lifted almost to her hairline.

"Of course, but I'm sorry to disappoint...again. There is nothing to check on." Keeping her face expressionless, Artemis stood still, facing her father's consort. Ivy lived on gossip like the rest of them lived on air.

"Oh, get your nose out of the clouds, girl, I mean you no harm!" Ivy's words sounded condescending. Artemis's hackles went up, and it took everything she had to remain calm.

"Be that as it may." Artemis stepped through the door and locked it behind her. "I must leave now, so I don't have time for pleasantries. Another day, maybe." She smirked as she walked past Ivy, leaving her standing at the locked door, her arms crossed over her chest and a frown on her face. "I have an arrow to find."

"We need to talk!" Ivy called after her, but Artemis just waggled her fingers over her shoulder and kept walking.

Some people's existence consisted of gossip and visiting. Fortunately for Artemis, her life had hunting, blood, and fighting. She wouldn't trade it for the worlds.

Chapter Six

Raphael barely noticed his surroundings as he zipped through the streets, everything blurring in his sight. His sleek, silver Aston Martin Valkyrie turned heads as soon as he slowed down, so he was trying his best to drive on roads that would have the least number of potential gawkers. Feeling the purr of the V12 engine behind him, made him feel exuberant. Having 1,130 horse-power under his hands was a new experience all on its own every time he slid into the soft leather seat of his favorite toy that could go from zero to sixty in two point five seconds. He loved his car very much but disliked the attention it received, even though he couldn't blame people for staring at it. It was his and he still stared at it most of the time. Shaking his head at his quirks, he started paying closer attention to his surroundings. According to his GPS, he should be close to the meeting place given on the coven's website.

The LA suburb was not posh, but not run down either —modern buildings surrounded by businesses and restaurants just like many other large cities. People milled around walking in and out of them; all apparently lost in their thoughts with their faces shoved in their phones — another thing that bothered him. No one made eye contact anymore. The connection you make with another being, even in passing, when your eyes lock for that split second was gone. Claude was telling him that he isolated himself, but according to Raphael, everyone was isolated but him. He just decided to watch from the sidelines as humanity destroyed itself slowly. They resembled machines more and more each day.

"You will reach your destination in five hundred feet." The disembodied voice of his GPS broke the silence.

"How very kind of you to notify me," Raphael replied dryly to the machine as he slowed the car to a crawl, looking for a place to park.

Nearing the front of what looked like a new age store, he was lucky to find one parking spot left with enough room front and back to keep his car safe from pathetic drivers. The world was full of them. He didn't concern himself much with humans, apart from satisfying his needs from time to time, so he would hate to kill a motherfucker now if they damaged his car.

Grabbing his suit jacket from the passenger seat, he opened the door and unfolded his six-foot-four frame from it. Putting the jacket on, he buttoned up his top two buttons with one hand as he pressed the lock button on his keys with the other, hearing the *'beep, beep'* sound. Striding towards the partially opened door of the store, he hoped that by some miracle, he would find at least a few solid answers here. It was highly unlikely, but Raphael always tried to look on the optimistic side of things.

The god-awful stench of too much incense hit him first, throwing his enhanced senses off-kilter before he felt the power of magic hit him full force at the center of his chest. A dizzying feeling made him stop just past the door and shake his head to clear it. It felt like he'd been punched, and all his other senses went on full alert. Coming here, Raphael was hoping to find information on the Fae. He had a sickening feeling that he stumbled onto something that, if it weren't for his dead friends, he would've left the hell alone without a second thought.

"Welcome to the House of Intuition. Is there anything I can help you with?" the woman who approached him, coming out from between two of the aisles, made him growl deep in his throat.

"You own this place?" Raphael snapped at her and winced internally at the tone of his voice. *Way to go, genius, scare her off before you get a chance to ask questions,* he thought to himself.

"And if I do?" She lifted an eyebrow at him "What are you, the IRS?" She eyed him up and down, and there was no mistaking the appreciation in her eyes.

Raphael knew very well that women—men as well for that matter—found him attractive. The way he looked was the reason he got shoved into immortality centuries ago, and nothing had changed to this day — neither his looks nor the people around him. Since he had no problem using it to get what he wanted, he turned on the charm. The woman was middle-aged and quite attractive herself, with long blonde hair and pale blue eyes covered by long lashes. Her hippie dress was hugging her curvy figure, accentuating her large breasts and round hips.

"Have you ever seen someone from the IRS that looks like me?" Raphael winked at her, and her pale skin darkened at her cheeks making him smile.

"I can't say I have, no." Her voice turned breathless as

she licked her lips. "Well, not with that kind of body, to say the least." She twirled a finger in his direction before locking eyes with him. "I'm Danny, but I'm not the owner. She's here, in the back. I can get her for you if you like."

"That would be most helpful, Danny." Raphael smiled at her, and she grabbed the shelf next to her. He wasn't sure if she was trying to hold herself back, so as not to come close to him, or he had pushed too hard with his charm and she was ready to faint. She had good self-preservation skills, whichever the case might be.

He watched as Danny strutted towards the back of the store, swinging her hips and looking over her shoulder a couple of times before she disappeared behind a black curtain. As soon as she was gone his smile dropped and he rubbed at his chest. What on Earth was going on in this place? He had felt magic before, many times, but the magic in this place had a punch that could bring a centuries-old, powerful vampire to his knees. For that reason alone, he didn't try to compel Danny to tell him what he wanted to know. One didn't stay alive this long by being careless or stupid.

"Know thy enemy; he might be a friend in disguise. If you know neither your enemy or yourself, you will succumb in every battle," he mumbled while pressing on his temples.

He felt that he might end up being the first immortal brought to death by a headache. Snorting at his thoughts, he opened his eyes only to have them locked with a piercing green gaze that gave him shivers. The woman standing in front of him watched him with her head tilted to the side as if she couldn't make anything of him. Looking like she was in her mid to late twenties, her beautiful face gave nothing away. Tall for a woman, her head came almost to his chin, and she watched him as he watched her. He was taking in the dark-as-night hair falling over her shoulders down to her waist, blending with the black flowing dress that reached the floor. A pentagram entwined with vines and leaves with three ruby stones in its center hung around her neck, falling between her breasts.

"You asked for me?" Her sultry voice made him focus on her eyes again. "How may I help you?"

"I'm looking for information on the Fae." Raphael decided to get right to the point, because she didn't look like someone that would appreciate small talk. "Dark Fae to be precise, and the Wild Hunt."

"Why are you wasting my time? We have books you can purchase, or you could google it." Both her eyebrows went up as though she was asking why he hadn't done that before coming.

"I can feel your magic." Raphael was irked by her condescending tone, so he snarled at her. "Don't you dare deny it, witch!" She closed her mouth as her eyes widened at his words. "You better start talking on your own, or I can make you."

"Vampire!" She hissed at him as her hands lifted from her sides, palms turned towards him.

"You can try it." Raphael tilted his head, his eyes flashing amber for a second as fangs poked from under his upper lip long enough for her to see them. "We can see who is faster."

"What do you want?" Dropping her hands limply to her sides, she looked wary.

"I thought I was clear."

"Information? That's all you want?" Incredulity was written all over her pretty face. Raphael just arched an eyebrow, making her narrow her eyes at him. "And if I tell you what I know, you'll leave? Not harm me or my coven?"

"You have my word!"

"Your word means nothing to me!" she snapped at him, "but your blood…that's a whole different matter." A smile lifted her full lips, making Raphael rethink his choices of trying to be nice.

"You'll never get anywhere near my blood, but my hat's off to you, witch. I must commend you for trying." Crossing his arms over his chest, he glared at her. "Now speak!"

After eyeing him for long moments, she slowly nodded her head as if agreeing with something in an internal debate. Taking a deep breath, she closed her eyes and released it slowly before looking at him again.

"If it's information you want, I don't have to tell you anything, vampire." As Raphael opened his mouth to say something, she lifted her hand, stopping him. He didn't miss the sigils painted in the center of her palm that were not there a moment ago. "I don't have to tell you anything because I will show you."

With those words, she turned on her heels and started walking towards the black curtain, leaving Raphael stunned for a second. She would show him? Why is everyone showing him shit he really doesn't want to have anything to do with? And show him exactly what? He had a very uneasy feeling about the whole thing, but his feet followed her of their own accord. Raphael just hoped he didn't get to meet any Fae face to face until he knew more about them. Know thine enemy and all that shit.

Chapter Seven

Stalking through the halls of the palace undetected was one of the most fun things Artemis had to do, because she had found it very informative from an early age. The things you see or hear, sometimes, were priceless. Most stayed out of her way because they knew she was more powerful than them, while others stayed away because they thought her a monster. It suited her just fine to have all of them to leave her alone. She didn't want any destruction.

"Feed your focus, woman. Don't get sidetracked." she whispered under her breath as she neared the Hall of Portals on silent feet.

Walking through the arched doorways, she stopped for a moment to look around as always. This room was the last part of her home her mother had seen before she departed this life. It was the last place Artemis could stop for a second and send her power out through all the empty portals in hopes that maybe one of them would open beyond space and time and her mother could feel the love Artemis carried in her heart for her. Every time there was no response, not even a flicker, but it didn't stop her from trying.

Bringing her focus back to the present, she walked up to the ornate frame of black obsidian, the one that leads to the human realm that had been closed to them for centuries until one day long ago, when it started to flicker slowly. It was a joyous day of celebration for everyone—except Artemis. She was ready to tear through it and level the realm to the ground—humans, vampires and their damned Earth alike. She was punished that day, punishment that took three turns of the sun to heal. Artemis still believed it was worth it and she would do it again if she had it to do over. Since that day, her father had been more determined to feed her anger. He might as well, because she could use it. In her mind, the only good human was a dead human, and the only vampire worth anything was dead. Their time would come, and she was looking forward to it.

Her waiting over, she shifted to her other form and stepped through the portal. Artemis had tried many times to pass through the portal in her human form, but it always stood as solid as a wall in front of her, while in her shifted form it let her glide through like through molasses. Shivers passed down her spine as she traveled from her realm to Earth. Stepping out, she found herself in the same woods like before. There was no storm this time, and the waxing moon was hanging in a cloudless sky like a decoration. It was brighter now than the night when she'd lost her arrow, and Artemis looked around. She noticed the trees swaying gently on the breeze and the sounds of animals scurrying around as well as owls screeching from a distance. Seeing it like this, it wasn't that bad of a place, she supposed. The colors appeared muted and the air smelled funny to her sensitive nose, but apart from that it was not that bad at all.

Venus Trap

Shifting back to her human form, she walked toward the last place she remembered being. It didn't take her long to find the spot, but there was no sign of her arrow anywhere. Frowning, she moved this way and that with the same result. The stench of a vampire was heavy in this spot, but what got her attention was the mixture of them. It could only mean that others had come and stood on this spot. Her senses were stronger in her other form, so she didn't waste time shifting and following the scent of bloodsuckers. It led her to the edge of the woods, where she had to stop to make sure nothing caught her off guard. Beyond the trees was a small field, and across it some type of flat rock cut through, making her scrutinize it. Cocking her head, she tried to decipher the buzzing sound coming from a distance that sounded more and more like a roar the closer it got. One of her legs was stepping out of the woods when two bright lights split the darkness, and flinching, she retreated fast in the cover of the trees. Her eyes widened as some contraption moving at a fast speed almost flew by, making her cringe from the loud noise it made before it was gone. *What in the fates was that?* A frown made a furrow between her brows.

Her eyes flicking from side to side, she waited for a little while, but when no other strange things showed up, she decided to keep following the scent before it disappeared. Artemis was almost halfway towards the strange flat rock when she stopped looking down at herself. She could move faster in her shifted form, but she would also stand out more if more of those things came out of nowhere, and flying was not an option if she needed to sniff the vampire stench in the air. Lifting her head, she took a long breath, determining which way to go before shifting back to her human form.

"Blending in is the best form of action right now," she mumbled as she headed in the direction of the scent.

The further she went, the more she realized how different this realm was. It was nothing like her home, and what was worse, it looked like the humans were destroying nature everywhere they could. Her anger kept building at what she was seeing. Her narrowed eyes were darting left and right, trying to take it all in. Savages, that's what they were. They were filth that thought themselves better than her kind. This realm should bless her for wanting to free it from them. As she neared some housing, she slowed down. There were a few smaller ones dotted around the area, but one stood out as more grandiose compared to everything else around it. Artemis knew the vampires were there, because she could smell them from where she was standing. There was a distinctive earthy smell to them mixed with coppery undertones that were unmistakable. Ignoring everything else, she walked right towards it.

As she neared the large ornate gates, she could vaguely hear the sounds inside, making her stop for a second to assess her next move. Reaching out her hand, she took hold of one side of the gate and wrenched it open before abruptly pulling her hand away, grunting in pain as her palm throbbed with a heartbeat of its own.

"Iron!" she hissed as she cradled her hand to her chest. "Of course they know that it will make us useless, so they hide behind iron." Pressing her lips together in a firm line, Artemis walked in and headed for the house on silent feet, shivering from the nearness of the stupid gate.

She debated whether she should go inside and clean the nest out or get inside unnoticed, retrieve her arrow and leave, as Lazarus expected her to do. Not that she listened often, but she knew those were his unspoken orders. By the time she reached the doors, she had decided it might not be smart to jeopardize their plans more than she already had, so, the plan was simple—go inside undetected, retrieve the arrow and leave the place, undetected.

"Simple," she whispered as she soundlessly opened the door and on silent feet, entered a house full of vampires.

She walked around the entire place with no one the wiser. Hiding in the shadows in the barely lit rooms and hallways, she heard useless talking, moans and groans that she ignored, but no matter where she looked, there was no sign of her arrow. Passing the third time along one of the hallways, she noticed that she had missed a door that seamlessly blended with its surroundings. Quite a large one to miss, and it only got her irritated. Grinding her teeth, she took hold of the double handles and opened it. The scent that hit her in the face was almost like a punch and it took her breath away. Quickly stepping inside, she pushed the doors closed and leaned her head back on it, closing her eyes and almost sliding to the floor.

Musky and inviting, it tied her stomach in knots and her legs grew weak. Breathing through her mouth, she lifted her head and looked around.

"A library…" her whisper trailed off as she looked around.

Nothing but books and a large desk with some thin silver box on it. What could affect her like this? Are they coming up with a weapon against her now? Is that what this was? Maybe Lazarus was correct and she did screw up things for everything they had planned. Her revenge would not happen because she couldn't let things be, for once in her life.

"No," she hissed to herself. "I am stronger than whatever this is. I will ignore it if it kills me." Determination burned in her chest.

Breathing through her mouth, she searched the entire library, but the arrow was not there either. She was angry, mostly at herself, but she decided to blame it on the vampires anyway. Artemis left the large house and started walking back towards the woods. It might not be easy to find the arrow, but she would find it, she had no doubt about that. She was heading back home because she needed to tell Lazarus that the vampires have created a weapon against her or maybe their kind in general. She wasn't sure if it was deadly, but it sure as hell weakened her to a point where she could barely think. She would report to him, take her punishment and then look for her arrow again.

With head held high as was her way, Artemis took one long breath, steeling herself for confronting her father as she shifted and stepped through the portal. Nothing could've prepared her for what she saw on the other side. The one thought that kept screaming in her head was *Where in the fates' name am I?*

Chapter Eight

Raphael walked warily behind the witch. The pressure in his chest lessened a little, but it was still there, sitting like a boulder and preventing him from taking a full breath. His eyes trailed over her frame, trying to figure out what kind of a witch she was when abruptly they focused on her hands. As she was sauntering along, her arms swinging gently at her sides, her thumb kept rapidly moving from index finger to pinky and back as if she's counting something. His eyes narrowed.

"Where are we going?" Raphael broke the silence.

"You said you wanted to know about the Fae." Looking over her shoulder at him, she smiled, and the uneasy feeling in Raphael's stomach doubled.

It wasn't a pleasant smile. It was a knowing smile, and those green eyes looking back at him seemed ancient. Maybe even as old as he was, but that was impossible. He could smell the blood coursing through her veins, and it smelled human. The beat of her heart was stuttering like a butterfly, telling him that she was afraid of him no matter how calm and fearless she seemed on the outside. Only the powerful magic that was still prickling his skin was suggesting otherwise, and now that look in her eyes. His eyes slid back to her hands. There was something peculiar about what she was doing with her fingers; only he couldn't place it.

"That I did." Raphael's soft baritone hummed through the hallway and the skin on her arms pebbled. "Beware, witch. After that comment about wanting my blood, I assure you I have no qualms about ending your life and that of everyone else here if you are playing games. It's for you to decide what's worth dying for."

"Save your threats, vampire. I have no intention of dying anytime soon." Without turning back to look at him, she continued walking forward. "Iris."

"Excuse me?" She caught him off guard with that last word, and it took him a moment to ask the question.

"My name. It's Iris," she answered with a glance his way, slowing her steps.

"Raphael." He replied in kind, stopping next to her just as they reached a door at the end of the long hallway.

"Now that introductions are out of the way, I need to ask few things of you before we go any further." Raising her eyebrows, she waited until he inclined his head. "You will stand on the side and away from all that is there. No matter what happens or what you see, you will not get involved or move from your place." She started ticking off demands on her fingers, "Lastly, you will not speak. Not a word until we are back here. Do you agree?"

"What exactly do you have behind that door, Iris? If you want me to agree with your terms, I must know what I'm getting myself into." Raphael lifted a hand, stopping her from talking. "I don't need to know all your secrets, nor do I wish to meddle with you magic folk. I simply need answers, and that is all. How I get those is entirely up to you. It can be as nice as this conversation has been." He smiled as she narrowed her eyes. "Or we can make it hard, and as much as I don't like hurting humans, I would have no problem ending your lives. Are we clear?"

"Crystal," she growled through clenched teeth. "There is nothing that can harm you behind this door. We were about to perform a worship ceremony to our goddess before you came. You can sit and watch, but that is all. Sometimes a Fae may show themselves to us on these ceremonies, since my goddess is one of the hunt and she protects the woods, and if tonight is the same, you might see for yourself one of them. Is there something you want me to ask if that happens?"

"And I can't be the one asking because?"

"No man should be present for this ceremony, because the goddess is the one for maidenhood and does not allow males in her worship. Don't make me change my mind," Iris hissed at him, her eyes flaring in anger.

"Ask about the Wild Hunt." Her eyes widened comically at his words. "And why they're coming here now. We know they're coming, because they lost an arrow." He winked at her.

"The Wild Hunt..." her whispered words trailed off, but Raphael didn't miss the quickening of her heartbeat when he mentioned the arrow.

"Who do you pray to, witch? Why is your goddess connected to the Fae, apart from that bullshit story of the woods?" Raphael's words made her shake her head, and he could see her mind working behind her eyes.

"The Wild Hunt? That's why you're here?" Throwing her head back, Iris starts laughing "You should try finding someone that worships the Horned God, Raphael. The Wild Hunt is all male warriors."

"Be that as it may, I'll take what I can get." He glared at her. "Now answer my question."

"She is the goddess of the wildlife, hunt, and maidenhood, as I told you. You are in the wrong place. If you still insist on being here, you either agree to my terms or go back to wherever you came from."

"Very well. Lead the way." Realizing they would be standing here a long time if he kept pressing for answers, Raphael decided to go with whatever she said and see for himself. It's not like she could stop him if he decided to break her terms.

Iris looked at him for several moments before she clenched her teeth, jerked her head in a nod and turning around, grabbed the door handle. Raphael heard her mumbled words, "Goddess, help me," but ignored them. As soon as she opened the door, he went on full alert, only to stop two steps inside with confusion written on his face.

"Welcome to our ceremony," Iris said, loud enough to make him wince.

There were two young girls, around the age of ten, if Raphael had to guess, in long white dresses standing in the middle of what looked like a prayer room. With a glance, he counted 31 statues placed around the room as well. All but nine of them were silver. The remaining ones were gold, and all resembled the same figure. What got Raphael's attention was not the gold or the depicted character. It was the bow slung over her shoulder and the arrow in her hand. His eyes narrowed, but Iris was sternly pointing with her finger at the side of the room, so he walked that way while his mind was spinning. He felt it in his gut that he stumbled onto something here. He just had to stay calm until he saw it through to the end. After all this was over, he would have a long conversation with Iris, no matter whether she liked it or not.

Raphael watched as she embraced the girls and told them to take their positions in front of the sizable golden statue. His fangs burst through his gums as Iris lifted her hands and dozens of candles lit up at ones with a burst of flames shooting up. The wall crumbled under his hand as he gripped it, trying to control his instinct and not rip the witch apart. As he stood there panting, the two girls started twirling around and singing. Their angelic voices calmed him down enough to hear what Iris was saying.

"Sing and then dance the Arkteia. Do the She-bear dance for her. Please the goddess so she can bless you," Iris told the girls as she joined them in the dance.

Raphael started truly enjoying the sound of the two little girl's voices, and he was able to distract himself from the magic. A smile played on his lips as he watched them lift their hands and stomp around while giggling between verses. Raphael almost forgot why he was in that room and the answers he was seeking when the first pull in the center of his chest happened. He froze like one of the statues, only his eyes darting around. The second pull was much stronger, making him almost stumble even though his back was almost to the wall. The two girls and Iris kept singing and dancing until he felt the third and strongest pull of power, unlike anything he had felt, a second before an array of colors burst in the middle of the room. Blinded by its brightness, he had to keep his eyes closed longer than was comfortable. As soon as the light lessened, he squinted at what now looked like a portal that had opened in the middle of the room. Clenching his fists, he tried his best to control his anger so he didn't walk up and strangle the witch. The power and uneasiness he felt around him now was the reason why he stayed away from magic.

Unlike him, the two girls and Iris were excited more than anyone had the right to be. Or it might have been that Raphael was so pissed off that everything bothered him at that moment. Squealing and twirling, all three of them dropped to their knees and spoke just one word.

"Artemis!" three voices said in unison.

As Raphael lifted his eyes from the three females kneeling on the floor to the swirling portal, everything around him stopped. Looking back over the centuries, he couldn't remember one moment in his entire existence that he had been as terrified as he was the moment he set eyes on what walked through the portal. He tried to launch himself at it by instinct, but the damn witch must have anticipated him disobeying her wishes, because he found himself rooted to the spot. The only comfort he could gather was the fact that the creature didn't seem to notice him, either.

Chapter Nine

The first thing Artemis noticed was that this was not the room with portals in the palace. Second, it was a large room empty of everything but statues, candles, and three females that were kneeling on the ground, their foreheads touching the floor. She was unsure if she should entirely walk out of the portal, so only her two front legs were in that room while the rest of her body stayed between realms. Waiting there produced an unpleasant feeling, but this had never happened to her before, and she was cautious. When none of them moved and no one was there to attack her, she slowly proceeded forward.

Raphael was frozen in place by the shock as he watched the portal. At first, two legs stretched out of it and looked like they belonged to a giant insect that was coming through the portal. They were almost as long as his body and his instincts were screaming for him to attack or get the fuck out of there. He wasn't sure if he should thank Iris or kill her for making him immobile. As he watched, the creature slowly started to come the rest of the way through the portal. With the second set of legs came a torso and a head, but he couldn't look at it properly because the third set of legs came out, followed by a long tail. All his muscles coiled for an attack. Everything in him screamed danger. If he could have, he would've laughed at himself for wondering what could be more powerful than a vampire earlier that day. The ancient power coming from the creature was something he had never felt or heard about before. That power was pulling on a rope of energy that was somehow attached to his chest with such intensity that he almost felt faint.

"Who are you? Stand up and face me!" the voice was seductive and melodic that took Raphael by surprise. He jerked his head up from the exoskeleton of the creature and looked at the head.

While Iris and the two girls stood up and watched her with awe written on their faces, Raphael found himself stupefied. Forward from the abdomen of the creature, there was no thorax, but the upper body of a beautiful woman. Shaking his head, he wanted to punch himself. This creature could crush him with one of those legs, and he is gawking like he has never seen a pretty face in his life. If he were honest with himself, he'd admit that he hadn't seen as pretty a face like hers, but that was beside the point at the moment.

Unable to stop himself, he looked at her again, avoiding the lower part of her body. She had a toned bare upper torso and round breasts covered only with a corset that did nothing to make him dislike her. Slender arms were folded over her chest as a frown pulled her eyebrows low over her violet eyes. One side of her mouth was slightly lifted in a cocky smirk that made it look like it was a permanent state of her lips. Thin horns twisted somewhat at the tips suited her beautiful face perfectly. Thick violet hair, twisted like a rope, hung down her back and fell between twin sets of shimmering wings.

Frowning, he looked down at her exoskeleton and slowly followed it up to her head. The realization hit him like a ton of bricks, and all of his anger and instinct to attack fled, making him almost sag in his spot. A dragonfly. She was a fucking dragonfly, and definitely not one of those cutesy, pretty bugs, no. A dragonfly with enough ancient power to crush him where he stood without blinking an eye. A stunning one, if he allowed himself to admit it, but that was unimportant.

"We have been praying to you, goddess. You have finally come to bless us." Iris's words brought Raphael back from his thoughts.

Artemis didn't know what to make of the female standing in front of her. The two young ones were staring at her in awe and fear, making her want to turn around and walk back through the portal. She had never learned how to deal with younglings. Her nostrils flared as she detected the same scent like at the vampire house. Her stomach clenched, and she unfolded her hands, bending down at the waist to glare at the human in front of her.

"What else you have here apart from the younglings, human?" The softly spoken words made Iris take a step back. Her eyes widened in fear that the goddess could see the vampire, even after she placed her strongest concealment on him.

"Do you have a weapon? You think you can harm me?" Artemis hissed at Iris.

Raphael watched, fascinated, now that the initial shock had worn off and he almost felt sorry for the witch. At Artemis's question, Iris almost sagged in relief. A snort escaped him, and he regretted it the next second. At the sound, Artemis jerked her head in his direction. He knew she couldn't see him, or she would've attacked him by now. When she looked his way their eyes locked, and for the first time in centuries, he felt his heart stutter and thump painfully in his chest. Grateful to his enhanced senses, he watched her nostrils flare and her pupils dilate as she took a long breath. An unexplainable pull was telling him to go to her, but he resisted it with everything he had.

"I have no weapon here, and I only wish for a blessing. One of your protectors and ambassadors told me you would come when the time allowed. I have waited for this day a long time." Iris made a low bow, making Artemis turn her attention to the witch.

Raphael was finally able to take a full breath, and his mind started whirling with what all this could mean. Then Iris's words registered and he went on full alert, looking sharply at the witch. Just how many creatures had she summoned through the veil? Raphael started getting the feeling that Iris was more trouble than even he had thought.

"My protector? And ambassador? Pray tell, human,, who it was that was that helpful to you so that I can reward him or her." Artemis did her best to stay calm and not show the human how furious she was. Who dared to come here and speak in her name?

"The female did not promise, but the male did. He promised to take our prayers and worship to you as well. I heard you are pleased with the offerings." As Iris spoke, her cheeks darkened to deep red, making Artemis narrow her eyes.

"What kind of offerings, human?" she glared.

"The songs...the dancing..." Iris stuttered "He said they were fit for a goddess such as you."

"Describe him," Artemis snapped, dismissing the female the witch had mentioned, and Raphael hoped that it was not someone she knew. There was a promise of death in those jeweled eyes.

"He was very handsome..." Iris swallowed past the lump in her throat, feeling miserable. She hadn't envisioned meeting her goddess like this.

"Be more specific. My people all look alluring and tempting to you humans."

"He had blue eyes and black long hair." Taking a deep breath, Iris released it slowly, and Raphael noticed she was doing that strange thing with her fingers again. "His skin was like melted caramel..."

"No need for more description," Artemis growled, making Iris flinch back "I will make sure he gets rewarded, human. Have no fear." There was a dangerous glint in her eyes. "But what should I do with you? Huh?"

"I just wanted a blessing, but now I know you are not the goddess I thought you were." Iris lifted her chin and Raphael was impressed by the human. He wasn't sure he could've stood firm if he had been in her mortal shoes.

"I am not!" She purred. "I should snuff out your life." Artemis tilted her head to the side in a very inhuman manner. "I can feel you have power in you. It'll be tasty." She smiled at Iris.

"Just let the children go. You can do what you want with me if I have displeased you." Pushing the two girls behind her, Iris stood firm in front of Artemis.

"I have no use of the younglings. They can go." Artemis

waved her hand dismissively, still looking at Iris like she were a tasty morsel.

"Go. Go, find Danny and stay there." Iris pushed both girls towards the door, and whimpering, they bolted towards it, slamming it shut behind them. Turning around, she proudly faced Artemis and Raphael hoped the witch would release him so he could at least try to help her.

As Artemis's lips lifted into a predatory smile, Iris started moving her fingers in that strange manner even faster, making Raphael feel sorry for her. It must be a nervous quirk, he realized. Too bad he wouldn't be able to ask Iris all the questions he had in mind. There would be no answers for him here, apart from seeing the woman-creature tonight. He watched, unable to help, as things moved in slow motion. The pull Artemis tried on Iris's life felt like a bomb blast in his chest. Just as he expected to see the witch falling, Iris lifted her hands and threw them in front of her, towards Artemis. The magic blast was so strong it almost lifted Artemis off the ground when it threw her back through the portal just before it winked out of existence. When the portal vanished, Iris crumbled into a heap on the ground and Raphael was finally released from her hold. He was next to her in the blink of an eye, bending down to lift her in his arms. Carrying her, he bolted out of the room towards the store in hopes that Danny would know what to do. After he left Iris with the other woman, he walked outside the store without a word. His feet ate the distance to his car in no time and he flung the passenger door open. Leaning in, his chest heaving as though he'd run for miles, he opened the dashboard and stared at the arrow sitting unassumingly there.

Before Artemis disappeared through the portal, he saw the same arrows slung across her back. Do all Fae use same arrows, or had he accidentally found the one he had been looking for? Gripping the car with his hands almost unconsciously bending the metal, he pried his fingers open and slammed the door shut. He winced at the sound as though it were a physical pain. It wasn't his car's fault that he let the killer go. He was now more determined than ever to get his hands on the Fae, and he would get Iris to help, too.

Chapter Ten

Artemis flipped head over heels a few times as she flew back through the portal. Angry and disoriented as she hovered in the air trying to clear her head, she looked around. She wasn't mad that the human had dared to attack; she understood survival instincts better than anyone, and she appreciated a good adversary any day. She was angry because she didn't know how to go back through the same portal and continue what she had started. Her mind was working hard with possibilities of going to the human realm again when she heard noises coming from outside the portal room. Lowering herself to the shiny marble floor, she shifted back to her human form.

"I see you're back." His words proceeding him, Lazarus strode inside the room. "Did you find your arrow?" He glared at her as though she were his enemy, making her anger spike higher.

"I did not." She glared back, her eyes glinting with the ire she felt at that moment. "I came back to tell you news of the human realm before I go back to get it."

"So you know where it is, then?" Crossing his hands over his broad chest, Lazarus tried his familiar tactic of intimidation by rustling his massive dark wings.

"I know who took it. That's enough to go on to get it back." She lifted her chin, staring him down even though he was a head taller than her. "Shouldn't you be more interested about what I've found out? I thought you wanted to have no missteps in your plan."

"Watch your words, girl. You have done more than I can tolerate lately to alter my plans. Daughter or not, everyone must follow the rules. It's what has kept us alive and thriving for centuries." His words boomed and bounced off the walls, making it sound like it was vibrating in her chest.

Artemis glared at him but bit her tongue. He was right in one regard; it had been her actions that had created this mess for all of them, because she couldn't stay put. Her mind was working on how to tell him about what she had found out without being punished more harshly for it. If the vampires were making a weapon, it was because of the killing spree she'd been on for days—that and losing her arrow. She had thought herself invincible, and look where it had got her. Regardless, she still refused to apologize. Punishment sounded much better than admitting to Lazarus that she had been wrong. Or worse, that she was sorry. Because she wasn't sorry, not at all.

"I will take my punishment now, father." She sneered the last word, making him clench his fists so hard that his knuckles turned white.

"What of the news?" A venomous glint sparkled in his eyes, making her stomach twist into knots.

She relaxed her stance as she debated whether she should tell him the truth. Not because she was a coward and wanted to escape his wrath; she definitely was not. Artemis didn't want to recount everything she had found out because some twisted part of her wished to see him fail with his 'perfect plan.' It was a ridiculous thought, because she wanted the humans to suffer as much as Lazarus did, but it was there nonetheless. She decided to turn it in her favor for once, and the words that came out of her mouth surprised even her.

"There is a human who can alter the portal as we travel through it." She watched as a frown formed on his perfect face; so different from her own. "I was going in one direction, but she pulled me to another. And she has magic." Lifting her hand to stop him from speaking, she continued. "It's not very strong, so it begs the question how was she able to do that."

She watched him, still unnaturally as he was staring at her as though he was seeing her for the first time. Artemis didn't miss the slight stiffening of his wings at her words, so her eyes narrowed. Lazarus knew something about it, and she wasn't sure if she should call him out on it or just let this whole thing play out as it will. The feeling of wanting to keep her mouth shut solidified as she watched him transform from the arrogant venomous creature he was a second ago to the relaxed, laid-back king that most of the Fae thought him. He was hiding something, and she would be damned if she didn't find out what that was.

"A magic human that can alter a portal with one of us traveling through it?" One of his eyebrows arched. "That's preposterous!" He made a cutting motion with his hand, and her eyes tracked it. "It must've been a fluke, a glitch… whatever you may want to call it. No human has that much power."

And there it was said out loud, Artemis thought to herself. That same thing had been nagging her the entire time. *How did that human manage to pull me through the portal?* Her whole life she had been told that they were below the Fae. Pathetic little creatures with no magic but full of greed and envy. Lazarus never missed a chance to remind everyone that the only reason they had succeeded in banishing the Fae had been that there were too many of them, and they had gotten help from the vampires. This little misfortune of her losing the arrow had brought a lot of revelations that said otherwise. Doubts started eating at her, doubts about everything she had thought was the truth. Had she been lied to all her life? And if that was the case, what else has he been lying about?

As Artemis opened her mouth to say just that to his face and provoke his ire, Lazarus spoke again. "We can talk about this ridiculous matter later. Now it is time for you to take your punishment." A cruel smile bloomed on his handsome face, "Follow me." He turned around and strode out of the room without looking to see if she would follow.

Artemis followed. She had never shied away from accepting the consequences of her actions. She held everyone else responsible for theirs and didn't think she should be an exception. She would be well, she always was. After all, everyone knew Artemis was the strongest Fae, after Lazarus, in the whole realm. She felt that she was stronger than he, but she kept it to herself. There was no need to make him hate her more than he already did. She had a feeling that his excuse that she irked him because she looked too much like her mother, whom he missed immensely, was just another lie.

A deep, tired sigh escaped her lips as she followed him through the hallways and into the fighting arena. Of course this would be her punishment. What better way to satisfy Lazarus then let him watch her bleed? Or kill. He looked over his shoulder at her before veering right and heading to the elevated balcony so he could see the fights better. She ignored everything as soon as her boots hit the sandy grounds. Everyone was already there, the surrounding seats filled to the brim. Shouts and screams echoed as they saw her stride into the center. Before she got there, Lazarus's booming words stilled her steps.

"Leave the bow and arrows. No weapons allowed." He stood, staring down at her from his perch. "We don't want you losing another one of your arrows, daughter. Not before you find the missing one, anyway."

Gasps, then silence followed his words. He had never before spoken openly about why Artemis was punished. The reasons always got around through gossip, most probably thanks to Ivy. Artemis was not sure if this was because of the arrow or because she had mentioned the magic human. Her mind spun with the implications as she walked confidently to the side and gently pulled her favorite weapon off her body. Laying the arrows on the ground, her fingers trailed over the bow, finally dropping it next to them as she calmed her breath.

Shouts announced someone else entering the arena and Artemis cleared her mind. She could think about everything after she was done here. While she healed, she would let her intuition help her make sense of everything she's learned. Hopefully it will bring her some clarity or at least point her in the direction of some answers. Turning around, she saw that her first opponent was another warrior from the Hunt. She couldn't even remember his name, but she knew his face. His chiseled body moved fluidly towards her as muscles jumped and bunched under his exposed skin. Such a shame that she would have to mark his handsome face. She smiled predatorily as she looked at him through her lashes. Artemis stretched her fingers at her sides before clenching her fists. Walking up to the center of the arena to meet him, her smile never wavered. She watched his silvery eyes track her swaying hips as she approached him and lust flared bright for everyone to see. When she finally stopped a few feet away from him, he lifted his eyes to her face. Her smile grew and his eyes widened while his throat bobbed as he swallowed.

"Such a pretty face," she mused gently, making him take a step back "Such a shame I will leave my mark on it." With those last words, she jumped up, and kicking out her boot, she connected hard with his chest, sending him sprawling a yard away on his back in a cloud of dust.

Landing with bent knees, she straightened up and slowly walked towards him. He was trying to lift himself off the ground, shaking his head to clear it. When he saw Artemis nearing him, he scrambled up and took a fighting stance.

"That's much better." She praised him like she would a youngling. "Let us give our king the show he so desperately desires."

The opponent's screams were not heard for long before they were replaced with another's. And another's. And another's. Artemis didn't stop until she saw her last opponent. Her power was waning, she had blood running down into her left eye from the cut on her face and she was slowing down, but at that moment new strength cursed through her veins and her smile bloomed again.

"I was hoping you would face me here today!" she told him.

Chapter Eleven

After calming himself down by breathing the chilly night air, Raphael returned to the store. Without stopping, he walked through the curtain at the back straight to the room on the left where he'd laid Iris on a couch and left her with Danny. The witch was still as pale as a corpse and unconscious, while Danny was wiping her forehead with a wet cloth. When Raphael walked in, Danny looked up at him with sad eyes.

"I see she's not awake yet." Pulling up a chair next to the dingy couch, Raphael sat down, leaning his forearms on his knees and steeping his fingers.

"No, she's not." A sigh escaped Danny as she dropped the wet cloth into the bowl of water on the ground next to her feet. "It takes a toll on her when she uses a lot of magic. I sent the girls home with their mothers as well."

"And this happens often, I presume?" He tilted his chin towards Iris. Although his words were conversational, he saw the young woman stiffen.

"I have no idea what happened back there."

"I only asked..." Raphael started, but she cut him off.

"Nor do I care what happened, or what she does." Danny glared at him. "I work for her. This is my job, and all I want is to do it and go home. I don't need, or *want* to know what goes on behind closed doors."

Raphael eyed the woman speculatively. He knew that if he pushed, she would only clam up, but he wasn't sure how to handle the situation. His isolation gave him little opportunity to improve his interactions with humans. After her outburst, which almost made him laugh, Danny busied herself with changing the water in the bowl and replacing the cloth, ignoring him like he wasn't in the room.

Straightening himself up and leaning against the back of the chair, Raphael stretched his legs in front of him, crossing them at the ankles. lacing his fingers together at the back of his head, he pursed his lips. Playing nice with the human was taking him nowhere. He wanted answers, which he wouldn't get by her turning into a blubbering mess and telling him what he wanted to hear. A change of tactic was needed, but not one so drastic that he would need to start playing nursemaid if she began to faint or scream. A shudder racked his frame. Triggering a drama was not his favorite pastime. He didn't want her freaking out, but fear was a powerful tool to use. He should know; he'd used it for a long time before pulling himself back from everything.

One second, Raphael was leisurely stretched out on the chair, the next, he was looming over her one hand wrapped around her throat and a high-pitched scream ripped from Danny's mouth. His fangs were glistening and his eyes were like burning fires too close to her face for comfort. The bowl full of water dropped to the floor, shattering in a thousand pieces and soaking both their legs up to the knees. Fear made her freeze, staring at him like a deer caught in the headlights.

"I will ask the questions and you will give me the answers, human." His words were little slurred through the long fangs, making her shiver in fear.

"I-I... I don't know...any-anything" Danny stuttered through numb lips, looking at Raphael with wide eyes.

"Oh, but you do." He cocked his head to the side, and his eyes flicked from her face to her pulsing artery on her neck and back. "What type of magic is she using?"

"I d-d-don't know." Her teeth started chattering, and Raphael realized he might've gone a bit too far.

"I will not hurt you." Taking a step back, he made sure his fangs retracted and his eyes went back to their natural color while removing his hand from around her neck. "I have no time to play games. Tell me what I need to know and I will leave you alone. What type of magic is Iris using?" he looked at her expectantly.

"I honestly don't know." Still shivering, Danny gripped her trembling hands in front of her.

"What type of a witch is she?" Raphael was getting frustrated again.

"That is her story to tell, not mine." Taking a deep breath, the color started returning to Danny's face. "I'm neither a witch nor do I understand the types of witches. I'm very serious when I say that this is my job. It's not stressful..." her words trailed off, and she grimaced. "Well, it wasn't until today. It pays the bills. That's all I know and all I can tell you."

"And you want me to believe that she never talks about it or that you've never asked questions? "He folded his arms on his chest.

"I can't tell you what to believe." She kept looking at him warily.

"What is it that you want to know, vampire?" The tired voice was soft, but he heard her words.

"You're awake!" He whirled towards the couch, seeing Iris watching them with tired eyes. There were dark circles under her eyes like she hadn't slept for a year.

"And wishing I wasn't." Iris groaned as she swung her legs off the sofa.

"This is my cue to be gone!" Danny bolted out the door as fast as her feet would carry her. Raphael ignored her, staying focused on Iris.

"I'm assuming that asking you to open that portal again is out of the question, then?" He lifted an eyebrow.

"Why the hell would I want to do that? Were you blind? Did you not see what came out of it?" Iris glared at him as what little color she had on her face drained. "I was praying to a goddess. At first, I thought it was Artemis, with her bow and all. That was not a goddess, I assure you. Something is wrong, and I have a feeling I helped it unknowingly." Her chin dropped to her chest.

"Why are you doing these worship dances, anyway? What kind of a blessing are you looking for?" Raphael looked at her curiously.

Iris watched him for few moments as if weighing her options—whether she should trust him or not. The argument she had with herself was clear in her eyes as he watched her and waited. Grabbing hold of the sofa with both hands as if to ground herself, or maybe for courage, she nodded at him, confusing the shit out of him.

"Ever since I was a little girl, I've had these dreams..." At those words, Raphael snorted and Iris glared at him.

"Sorry." He cleared his throat, letting the expressionless

mask he usually wore take over his face. "Please, continue." He waved her on.

"As I was saying, I've had these strange dreams that didn't feel like dreams at all." Her eyes flicked towards him as if expecting him to interrupt her, but he waited patiently. "In those dreams, I'm in a beautiful room and everything is brighter, the colors are more vivid and the air feels like it's caressing your lungs as you breathe it. There is also a woman there. She's so beautiful that it hurts to look at her. She glows like the sun. That's why I thought I was praying to a goddess. She has been teaching me the dance, the songs...everything, really. She taught me all of it in my dreams. And every time, without exception, she would tell me, "Pray for Artemis, child. She is your salvation."" Iris stops her rambling and took a deep breath. "More like my doom, from what we know now, huh?" She looks at him sheepishly before dropping her head and looking at the hands folded in her lap now.

"I need to find that creature." Raphael spoke calmly, although his gut tightened at the thought of what he had seen and what she was telling him now.

"Why?" Iris lifted her head and looked at him through her hair where it had fallen over her face.

"She killed some of mine. I need her to pay for it."

"If you think any of us stand a chance against her, you are sorely mistaken." Her voice was a tired monotone. "No offense."

"None taken, but I do need to find her." Raphael didn't back down, although he was aware Iris spoke the truth. Everything in him screamed that he needed to find the creature.

"How do you know it was her that killed your people?"

She frowned at him. "I've never seen anything like her in my life."

"She had the same arrows as the one we found. It's definitely her." He was getting more confident by the second.

"You have one of her arrows?" Jumping off the couch, Iris swayed, and only Raphael's quick reflexes saved her from face-planting on the floor.

"Easy, witch. Yes, I have one of her arrows." He lowered her back to a sitting position.

"Can I see it?" Iris looked at him, her green eyes stark on her ashen face. Before she could blink, he was gone and back, making her hair fly around her face.

"Here it is."

With shaky hands, Iris took the arrow and examined it. Her fingers glided gently over it as she turned it around. Bringing it closer to her face, she looked closely at the intricate designs and symbols on it, seeing their faint glow sparkle everywhere her fingers touched. Lifting her index finger, she poked at one of the symbols and it gave her an electric shock, making her jump. Her eyes snapped to Raphael's. She stared at him for a long moment before deciding that she had to trust him. If what she suspected was in fact about to happen, she would need to trust someone, and the vampire was an excellent ally.

"I think you were right about the Wild Hunt." Taking a deep breath, Iris didn't take her eyes off his. "And they are trying to open the portal. The problem is…" She chewed on her lower lip. "I think I helped them."

"Can we stop it from opening?" Raphael had a horrible feeling about what her next words would be. He wasn't disappointed.

"No, we can't." Iris pressed her lips in a thin line. "But, I think I can bring her back again if I use this arrow as a beacon." She pointed it at him, making him jerk his body away from it.

"And how do you know this?" He narrowed his eyes as he pulled the arrow out of her hands. He should snap her neck. It was because of her that his friends were dead. He should do it, but he couldn't. He needed her help. Without it, they were all doomed.

"Because I use Fae magic. It has been through my lineage for generations. In my family, all women have the dreams." She lifted her chin proudly. "If we are going to bring her back, you had better be sure you can hold her without getting us all killed."

"And how would I accomplish this?" Both of Raphael's eyebrows went up mockingly.

"Iron, vampire. It weakens them a lot, and we actually might stand a chance to survive long enough to find out what is going on. You'll need iron. Lots and lots of iron." She smiled humorlessly.

Chapter Twelve

Anger bubbled up as Artemis watched her last opponent stroll towards her as if he expected to be the winner. There was an arrogance in his demeanor that she looked forward to squashing under her boots. She watched him approach, not letting the urge to wipe the blood off her face pull her focus away from him. She had enough time to calm her breathing before he stopped in front of her, cocking his head to the side.

"You okay?" A frown pulled his eyebrows down as Fern watched her.

"I'm very well, thank you." Artemis gave him a toothy grin, more a baring of teeth than a smile, before adding, "Protector...or should I call you Ambassador?"

The widening of his eyes, albeit barely perceptible, was all the confirmation she needed. She guessed correctly that he was the one going through the portal to be in contact with the human. The question burning inside her was, why? Why would he be in contact with a human, and especially in her name? Too many things started to make no sense.

Too many doubts and red flags began to fracture the firm convictions she had built her entire life around.

"We don't need to fight. Lazarus has already gotten his fair share of entertainment." Fern tried to change the subject, making her angrier. "And you have received enough punishment, if you ask me." He waved his hand, encompassing her disheveled appearance.

That was enough for Artemis. She struck like a snake. The heel of her palm connected with his chin, flinging his head back before Fern had time to blink. Multiple fast punches caved in his torso, making him grunt in pain, and a round kick sent him to the sandy ground with a clearly-audible thud. Flipping her braided hair over her shoulder, she walked up to him and stared him down. He was curling up with his arms wrapped around his stomach, struggling to lift himself up. She might have sent some of her power in her hits, but it was part of her, not a weapon. At least in her book it wasn't.

"How is that for someone that has had enough punishment?" she spat at him. "But worry not, Protector. I have plenty more where that came from." She sneered as she bent down to look at him, her hands on her hips.

"There is no need for this, Artemis." Fern coughed as his face twisted in pain. "I can explain…"

"Why is it that you always have things that you need to explain to me, Fern?" Straightening up, she placed her boot on the side of his face, pressing just hard enough that he let go of his stomach so he could try to push her foot away. "Have you ever asked yourself why that is? Huh?" Through clenched teeth, she pushed the words out.

"There are things that I cannot say since I have given my vow. You know I can't break an oath to our king. You have made them, too," Fern grunted in pain.

"You have made an oath not to tell me things?" Removing her foot, she grabbed hold of his hair and lifted his head. "What is so important that he doesn't want me to know? Speak!" She shook his head.

Fern just pressed his lips into a firm white line and scrunched up his eyes. He wouldn't even look at her, and it made her even more angry. He was the closest thing to a friend she had, and here she was tempted to end his life right there in the middle of the arena. Rage burst through Artemis at the thought of anyone manipulating her, and it distracted her long enough that she was caught off guard when Fern twisted his legs around and flipped her onto her back. Straddling her waist, he trapped her arms with his legs. Leaning down, his hair, now released from the tie that had held it, hung over them like a curtain, shielding both their faces from view.

"Don't fight me on this, Artemis, it's what he wants," he hissed at her. "There are things that I don't even know, but I'm trying to find out. I can't do that if he doesn't trust me."

"Things like what, you two-faced snake? Like the lies you have all been feeding me?" She laughed without humor. "Oh, yes. I'm onto your plotting and betrayal. When I find out exactly what it is, there will be no place for you or him to hide."

"Keep all that to yourself, Artemis. Things are not as we have thought. There are hidden agendas behind his plan to attack the human realm. Armies are training out of sight." Fern pretended like he was struggling to hold her down, making her frown at him.

"I'm leading the armies, Fern, that's not hidden from me. Stop trying to manipulate your way out of this." Using her power, she flipped him over her head and jumped up. "The time for talking is over."

She kicked him, raising him off the ground and sending him tumbling away from her. She watched him slowly turn onto his side and raise up on one elbow as he coughed out blood. The ground blackened where the drops fell. Artemis walked towards him with hesitant steps.

"Stand up and fight me, you coward!" she growled through clenched teeth.

"I will not fight you. I told you that." Fern coughed up more blood. "You are not my enemy."

"No, but since you're plotting against me, you're mine." She glared at him while wondering why he kept coughing up blood. She hadn't hurt him that badly. "What's wrong with you? You've grown weak!" she spat at him.

"Things are not the way he tells them, Artemis. Watch your back. "He kept coughing while the sandy ground around him turned darker still from the blood. "Talk to…" Another coughing fit racked his frame and cut off his words.

"Talk to whom?" She dropped to her knees next to him and grabbed his shoulders, not caring who saw her. "Talk to whom, damn you!" She shook him, but his head lolled to the side as his eyes closed and didn't open.

At that moment, everything around her burst to life, making her heart skip a beat at the sheer volume of the noise. Artemis realized that Fern had used his power to mute their conversation just as he had muted the sound of the full arena that was echoing with screams and cheers of her name. She ignored it all as she watched a stream of blood trickle from his slightly parted lips down his chin to his neck. It was incomprehensible to her how she had hurt him so badly. She didn't use that much power nor that much strength in her hits. Then it hit her—the oaths. He has broken an oath and it was killing him. Her mind worked frantically, trying to think of a way to help him. She needed answers and he was the only one willing to give them to her, even at the cost of his own life. She needed to find Ivy, but before she could even try to lift him up and search for the consort, there was a strong pull at the center of her being, making her curl over Fern's immobile body protectively. A second pull followed, feeling like someone was trying to turn her body inside out, and she grunted in pain. The third was so painful that an involuntary scream ripped from her throat just before she realized that she was about to be pulled through a portal that had materialized right next to her. At the last moment, just before she was yanked into it, she grabbed hold of Fern and they both blinked out of the arena, followed by the livid roar of Lazarus. It was the last sound she heard before she lost consciousness.

Chapter Thirteen

Iris looked around the woods where Raphael had brought her. She still couldn't understand why they couldn't just work at the back of the store. Frowning, she kept checking every shadow that seemed to come alive under the light of the moon that was hanging like an ornament on the cloudless sky. The air was crisp and it smelled like snow. Winter was nearing, and she could feel it as it pebbled her skin. She was rubbing her hands over her arms to warm them up a little, turning in slow circles. Iris kept wondering where Raphael was, if only to keep her mind occupied with something. Her question was answered as she heard branches breaking and a lot of cussing coming from a distance. The trees were swaying and bending as though a herd of elephants was stomping through the woods, making her heart speed up. *What on Earth is going on?* she thought to herself just as the tree closest to the clearing bent almost in half before breaking.

Iris jumped a foot off the ground as the fallen tree thumped, then rolled few yards away from her. A very feminie squeak escaped her as a monstrous contraption pushed its way towards the clearing, and she clamped her hands over her mouth. It took her a moment to see what it was and her hands dropped to her sides as her jaw dropped to her chest.

"Wow!" she told Raphael when she finally saw him striding towards her like he was having a casual walk, not carrying a cage that could fit a dinosaur. "Where the hell did you manage to find this thing?"

Dropping the cage in the center of the clearing, Raphael ignored her while he spoke softly to the three vampires that were helping him. Their eyes kept flicking towards her before they left in a blink of an eye. He strode around the cage inspecting it and even grabbed the bars to shake it as if checking its sturdiness, making Iris snort. Well, her question didn't get his attention, but that snort sure did.

"You find something funny, witch?" He glared at her. "This had better work, or I'll keep you in this cage and use you as a personal blood bank."

"If it's iron, it will hold her. Iron weakens the Fae; it's the only thing we can use against them, as I told you. Where did you find it, or you have cages stored just in case?" She shuddered at the idea of being kept in a cage, then guilt started eating at her because that was exactly what she was going to do to another living being.

"There's a circus in town. You'd be surprised what humans are willing to do if you offer enough money. Let us get it done, then. The sun will start coming up soon, so we don't have much time." Crossing his arms over his chest, he stood there staring at her expectantly.

"Right-o, boss man!" Iris mumbled under her breath as she started grabbing the pillar candles and positioning them around in a circle.

"Vampires have very sharp hearing, witch. Less mumbling, more doing." He smirked when she glared at him over her shoulder.

Iris decided to ignore him as she got herself ready to summon the owner of the arrow. She picked up the bundle that she had placed on the ground when she got to the woods and unwrapped the arrow. Reverently, she took the object and set it on the grass before sitting cross-legged facing it. Raphael watched her as she closed her eyes and her thumb started moving again from index to pinky and back in rapid succession. Frowning, he watched as shadows jumped and danced over her pretty face as she hummed softly under her breath. Her humming grew slowly louder, and Raphael leaned his back against the cage, crossing his legs at the ankles, waiting. He was coiled like a spring, ready for the creature to show up so he could somehow guide it inside the cage—if it didn't kill him first.

"That's done. Now to summon the Fae." Iris's words made him frown.

"What's done?" he asked her.

"Oh, I just cloaked the cage. We don't want her angrier than she will already be when she sees it."

"Smart thinking," Raphael mumbled, impressed by the way she always seemed to think ahead and make sure nothing happened that she wasn't prepared for.

"I have my moments." She glared at him again before closing her eyes. "Now keep quiet and let me do my thing. Be ready to get out of the way when she comes at you. If you don't lock that cage, we're both shish-kebabs. Well, you'll be that anyway, when the sun comes up. Extra crispy." Iris snorted at her joke, making Raphael's lips twitch involuntarily. Clearing her throat, she started humming again, and her thumb started the same motion, making Raphael even more curious about it. He decided to ask her about it after he had the creature trapped.

Before long, sparks like tiny fireworks started sparkling in the middle of the clearing. He watched, ready to spring into action in the blink of an eye as the flashes turned into little explosions of light before starting to swirl together. Iris's humming grew in volume, and as she got louder, the swirling colors in the clearing got larger, reacting to her voice. Raphael had to admit, if only to himself, that he was in awe of the witch. He didn't know many magic users, but he had a feeling she was powerful in her own right. His mind got snapped out of his thoughts as all the swirling colors connected, forming a giant ball of rainbow colors in the middle of the clearing. His hands clamped over his ears as a mind-blowing roar echoed from the portal a second before something hit him in his chest and he tumbled into the cage with it.

Pulling himself away from twisted limbs, Raphael finally managed to untangle himself and stand up. It took him a moment to understand what he was seeing. A woman and a man were tangled together, and they both looked like someone had used them as a punching bag. He could barely hear the man's heartbeat, but the woman's was even and calm, as though she was sleeping. Bending down, he tried to separate them so he could see who the hell they were.

"What the fuck did you pull here, witch! This is not the creature..." Raphael's words were cut off as a hand wrapped around his wrist in a firm grip. Looking at his wrist, his eyes followed the arm up to a bloody but still beautiful face. Her eyes opened, and he would never forget those eyes in his life. *How is it possible that she looks human?* Her words stopped any further questions and shocked him more than anything so far.

"Help him." Sultry whispered words reached his ears, making chills run down his spine. "Please…" she begged him with her words and her eyes before they rolled to the back of her head and she went limp.

"Is that…" Iris stood behind him bending down to look over his shoulder. "Is that her?"

"It is." Raphael couldn't take his eyes off the woman in front of him. "Yes, it is," he repeated. more to himself than Iris.

Chapter Fourteen

"Are we going to sit and stare at her until she wakes up, or are we going to kill her?" Claude's angry words brought Raphael back from his thoughts while he was looking unblinkingly at the woman ever since they had brought the cage, with her in it, to the mansion. He rubbed the center of his chest absently. "And before you start giving lectures, let's not forget that she killed four of ours already. Our friends, need I remind you! I'm not planning on testing the durability of that iron cage." Flinging his hand towards the cage, Claude started pacing.

"Calm down, Claude. She's not going anywhere. Iris said the iron will hold." With a tired sigh, Raphael pushed himself upright, away from the wall he'd been leaning on.

"What? All of a sudden, you trust a witch that you just met today?" The glare that Claude sent his way would've made anyone else rethink their next words. Raphael never had a problem disappointing Claude and his expectations.

"Yes." He didn't feel like explaining to Claude that there was something about Iris that from the start, made him want to trust her. After she sent the creature through the portal with her magic, he didn't need more convincing. *The enemy of my enemy is my friend* was the way he looked at it—not that Claude needed to know that.

"Yes? That's all you have to say? You don't even trust *me* most of the time and I was there to make sure you stayed alive when you went after Anissa. I stood against our maker for you!" Claude's voice was getting louder with each word spoken while his eyebrows hit his hairline as he widened his eyes in incredulity. "I have people here that depend on me for protection, Raphael! I will not let you think with your dick at the expense of their lives—or mine, for that matter!"

"Think with my dick? Is that what you think I'm doing?"

"You haven't blinked or moved from that spot ever since we brought her here. Want to share why that is? I'm sure it's not because you've never seen a woman before." Still glaring, Claude crossed his arms over his chest.

Another sigh escaped Raphael as he rubbed his hands over his face. Claude was not far off with his remarks about the gist of it. There was something about the woman in that cage that pulled at Raphael so fiercely that he couldn't bring himself to harm her, and he hated it. He was aware of how ludicrous it was to now have the urge to protect the one he wanted to kill, mere hours ago, but the longer he looked at her, the more convinced he became that there was more to the story. Something wasn't adding up, and his gut feelings had never guided him in the wrong direction. Well aware that he should just end her life while she couldn't shift into the creature he saw at Iris's coven, he still hesitated. The time when he made snap decisions was behind him. He had made more than enough mistakes by acting impulsively to last him a few more centuries. He had a nagging feeling that there was more to this situation and he wanted to solve the puzzle that was the woman curled up, sleeping innocently in his cage.

Raphael remembered a time long past when he'd been held in a dungeon much smaller than the iron cage in front of him. The pain and humiliation he'd felt as he was used for his blood and his body by his maker before she turned him, when he tried to end his life, were causing bile to rise in his throat even now, centuries later. Claude could never understand what it felt like to be made to do things at another's whim, beyond your control. He willingly accepted his immortality and played along with Anissa's twisted ideas of fun. But Raphael knew. Oh, how he remembered. He would not do it to another living being, no matter the cost.

"So you're just going to ignore me?" Claude's persistent chatter, combined with the memories he tried to push back to wherever they'd been buried until he got here, started getting on Raphael's nerves.

"Don't you have something better to do?" He started pacing himself. "No one is doing anything until she wakes up! If anyone tries, they'll have to go through me first!" The words were spoken with a finality in them that would brook no argument.

"Listen to me, and listen well!" Claude got into his face. "If she moves one hair out of that cage, *both* of you will pay for it. Am I clear?"

"Haven't you learned that threats don't sit well with me, old friend?" Deceptively calm, Raphael straightened, smiling in a way that made wariness creep up into Claude's eyes. "I don't give a fuck how you treat the rest of your court and I have not gotten involved with it. But be careful who you provoke, Claude. You're frightened. Trust me, I get it, more than you think." Lifting a hand, he stopped the rebuttal that was about to come. He continued, "Only a moron would not fear what we have come across, if he wanted to live. I feel that same fear, too! But this is not an animal. Think about it for a second." Tapping his temple with his finger, Raphael stared intently at Claude "Don't you want to hear what made her come here and start killing us? Why, after not being seen for centuries, do they come now?"

"If we kill her, we don't have to worry about it any more!" Claude snapped stubbornly.

"Really?" Sarcasm dripped from Raphael's words like honey. "Because if she's dead, others won't come? That's how delusional you are?" The barely-perceptible shifting of Claude's eyes brought every instinct he had to full alert. "You know something you're not telling me!" he snarled angrily.

"Who's delusional now?" Throwing both hands in the air, Claude stormed past him, heading for the door. "You've lost your mind while locking yourself away from everyone. If you keep it up, we might need to put you down alongside Anissa!" With one last glare over his shoulder, he walked through the door and slammed it behind him.

Raphael stood frozen in his spot, not taking his eyes off the door. Claude was hiding something. It wasn't just a gut feeling telling him that. He has known the vampire king for a very long time, and every time Claude didn't want to share information, he'd walk away from an argument, like he'd done just now. What could make him want to kill the Fae before she wakes up? He knew that his friend wanted to have an advantage in all situations. So what made him refuse to have it now?

Turning around, Raphael looked at the woman again. She seemed small and harmless, curled up in the corner of the large cage. An overwhelming need to protect her took over his thought process again. Maybe Claude was right and he had lost his mind. But be that as it may, he still felt that he needed to get to the bottom of this, even if it cost him his immortal life. Determination burned strong in him, and he knew he would do anything to see this through.

Walking up to the cage, he crouched down and reached inside. Gently, with just two fingers, he moved an escaped tendril of her hair away from her face. It was silky and soft and it slipped through his fingers a few times before he managed to move it. Her eyelashes fluttered and he held his breath, thinking she might wake up. After a few moments, he realized she was probably dreaming and he released the air from his lungs. The smell of cypress filled his nostrils, and he couldn't stop the groan that rumbled deep in his chest. She was awakening things in him that he thought were long dead. Yet instead of turning around and walking away, leaving Claude to do as he wanted, Raphael stayed there, watching her as though mesmerized. To make matters worse, he knew he would stand guard like he was her personal watchdog until she woke up. That thought didn't unsettle him as much as he thought it would.

Chapter Fifteen

Stretching her arms over her head, Artemis winced at the pain that shot through her entire body. With a groan, she curled up on her side, cursing softly at the fates. Wondering why she felt like something had chewed her up first and spat her out later, she tried to open her eyes, but only one responded. The other managed a sliver, but she closed it immediately because of the throbbing pain she felt. Her mind was working furiously to figure out why she was feeling like that. Before she could do that, however, she noticed a few things she'd overlooked when she woke up.

The first thing was that she wasn't in her bed, because she was curled up on top of something scratchy on a hard floor. Second, she could smell vampires. Not one or two, but *many* of them. She remained motionless, straining her ears to hear anything that might tell her what is going on. As if invited, the memories from the day before rushed in like a flood. Her search, the arena, Lazarus and last Fern and his unresponsive body after telling her about armies that she knew nothing about. As if that weren't bad enough, now she was somewhere surrounded by vampires. Lately it had seemed like things were spiraling out of control and hitting her one after another, without a break. *Is this what they mean when they say the road becomes more difficult the closer you get to the truth?*, she thought to herself. The next second, she rose abruptly to her knees, forgetting all about the pain she was in.

"Fern?" she called out, her voice rough from sleep. "Fern, where are you?"

As she finally looked around her, everything froze in her mind. Her heart sped up and she could feel her blood rushing through her veins. Everywhere she looked, all she could see were bars. Bars and bars of iron, all around her. Clenching her fists, she glared with her one good eye at the iron as if it were its fault that she was surrounded by it. Beyond that were only brick walls and a disgusting smell that was making her nose twitch.

"Where in the fates' name am I again? This is getting ridiculous!" she mumbled, just as she heard the low screech of a door opening somewhere behind her.

She smelled him before he even walked through the door. Unable to control herself in the rough state she was in, Artemis hissed as she swung around, looking for the vampire. Her eye locked on grey ones full of anger and malice. There was hunger there, too, sending her rage to a new level of crazy. Without thinking, her body lifted and shifted to her other form and she looked down from her height to find the vampire backing out of the door, pure terror written all over his face.

"Aww, are you going to run now?" she mocked him. "I thought I was locked in here because you wanted to play." Pouting and tilting her head, Artemis baited him, trying to get him to come closer. If only she could get her hands on him...

Her trick might have worked, judging by the anger that made his eyes burn red, but there was a barely perceptible movement outside the door and that scent of a musk, from something she couldn't name that they used as a weapon on her, hit her full force. Her body shifted back to her human form on its own accord and she dropped to her knees, panting. Something was terribly wrong with her. It was either the iron, the weapon they used on her or being summoned through a portal in her human form. That was her first time passing through a portal like that, and it was the most logical conclusion. A thud was heard a second before the door opened fully, and the vampire was shoved inside the area where they kept her, stumbling and flailing his arms to stand upright.

Raphael saw the young vampire trying to get inside the garage that he'd had to use to keep the cage. Maybe he should've stopped the youngster, but curiosity got the better of him and besides, he wanted to see the reactions of both the vampire and his prisoner. He heard her awaken and talk to herself but had waited to see if he would find something useful in her mumblings. When the coward tried to run, he grabbed the kid by the scruff of his neck, and after smacking him into the wall, Raphael shoved him inside the garage. Taking a deep breath and putting his hands in his pockets, Raphael walked in as nonchalantly as he could manage. He was dying to see her again. She was terrifying in her shifted form, but as a human? He felt spellbound by her and her beauty. Even battered and bruised, she was the most beautiful woman he had seen in his long life. That contrasted massively with the terror he felt from the enormous insect she could turn into and with the knowledge of what she is capable of. Still, he found himself pulled as if by an invisible thread towards her.

"Lurking in the hallways like a creep," he mumbled, admonishing himself as he walked through the doorway.

"I was just checking that everything was good and secure here." Misunderstanding Raphael's words, the young vampire started explaining himself while trying his best to ignore the woman on her knees in the cage, glaring daggers at them with only one eye. It was quite impressive.

"I'm sure you were." Raphael's voice was soft; his words cultured. He noticed her shivering at the sound of his voice, and for some reason it made him feel good. *I really am thinking with my dick! What the hell is wrong with me?*

The woman seemed to forget all about the other vampire. Her eye was tracking Raphael, and it made him realize how focused and good her instincts were. She knew he was the more significant threat, so he held all her attention while she dismissed the less-powerful male in the room.

Artemis watched the bloodsucker walk inside, and she couldn't help but admire the masculine beauty before her while she hated herself for even noticing it. His dark brown hair was cut short at the sides but left longer on top, styled nicely to stay off his forehead. Green eyes stole glances her way, making her heart skip a beat each time they made eye contact. There was a tightness around his mouth, making his full lips look firm. Dressed in some fancy clothing, his jacket was pushed aside, revealing a button-down shirt stretched over impressively firm chest as he kept his hands in his pockets. Shiny black shoes poked from under the pants that were hugging his thighs and backside like they never wanted to leave his body. Artemis glared at him, more because she was angry at herself. This was her enemy, and she should be plotting his death, not looking at him as a male and admiring his perfection. And he *was* perfect. It must be that scent messing with her mind, she decided. This was not normal behavior. It took her a moment to realize that he was talking to her.

"What is your name?" Raphael asked her, unable to help himself.

He didn't receive an answer. She didn't break eye contact or move a muscle. Still kneeling on the floor, she stared unblinkingly at him. Raphael tried to look for any clue that she was nervous, or possibly even scared about being locked in a cage, but he found nothing of the sort. Not so much as a muscle twitched on her feminine body.

"I know you understand me, I've heard you speak before today," he tried again, and this time he got a reaction.

Her good eye widened subtly in surprise but narrowed down at him suspiciously a second later. Raphael winced internally at his big mouth. He didn't want her to know he'd been there when she met the witch. Not yet, anyway.

"You spoke when you got to this realm and again when you woke up," he said, trying to remedy the situation since he couldn't pull the words back.

The narrowed-eye look didn't waver. Then in a split second, her eye jerked to the side and back towards him. It made Raphael realize he'd forgotten all about the other vampire. Before she could blink, he had the young vampire by his neck and pushed his face between the bars of the cage.

"Is this what you want?" he asked her, not letting go of the wiggling vampire who was yelling, begging to be released. *What a blubbering fool,* Raphael thought to himself.

She watched Raphael's face for a moment as if judging his sincerity or his sanity. Just as Raphael thought she would stay motionless like a statue, she struck like lightning. One second she was on her knees sitting docile while glaring at him, the next she had the young vampire around his neck and twisted his head three hundred and sixty degrees. Raphael opened his mouth to tell her that vampires can't be killed like that, but he left it hanging open when she twisted again and separated the head from the body without breaking eye contact with him. Thick coppery blood sprayed all over both of them and as he watched her bathed in blood, something primal awoke in him. He realized he wanted her more than he had wanted anything in his immortal life—and here she was, ready to kill him the first chance she got. The irony was not lost on Raphael, and then she spoke, making his gut tighten in response.

"Artemis. That"—a wicked smile lifted the corners of her plump lips—"is my name, bloodsucker." A voice out of his wildest dreams purred at him as she lifted her arm and wiped the back of her hand over her mouth.

Chapter Sixteen

Raphael wondered for the upteenth time if it had been way too long since he looked at a woman for more than quick relief. Maybe that was the reason why he wanted to open the cage door and bury himself so deep inside her that he'd be hard pressed to distinguish them as separate beings. Still, eyes locked with hers, he was trying very hard to stay calm and collected instead of acting on his desires. Artemis hadn't moved, either. Standing close to him, only the iron bars separating them, assessing him.

"Raphael." His name slipped from his lips, making a shiver run down her spine at the sound of his voice.

Artemis watched him, unable to move away or turn around, even when the iron bars were slowly leaching out her power. It bothered her greatly that she felt more towards him than just hatred for his kind. What was it about him that made her stomach churn and her legs to want to shift uncomfortably in his presence? She stayed where she was, afraid that if she moved she would give away her weakness. That scent that was making her dizzy was much stronger, now that he was almost in arm's reach.

Slowly, as if expecting her to bite his hand off, he reached through the bars and ran the back of his fingers gently over her face. Instinctively she flinched at his movement and his hand froze, but she didn't miss the twitch of the corners of his lips. It made her furious with herself.

"Who did this to you?" Reluctantly, Raphael pulled his hand back.

She didn't answer him, and he wasn't expecting her to. At his words, she retreated farther into the cage, still tracking him with her eye. The other looked painfully swollen, and Raphael wanted to do anything to make it feel better so he could feel her beautiful eyes on him. He shook his head at his thoughts, making her frown.

"So, you're going to just sit there and not talk to me?" With a sigh, he took a step back, pulling a handkerchief from his pocket and started wiping the blood off his face. "I need answers, and it seems you're the only one that can give them to me." Looking down at the cloth in his hand, he grimaced. Tossing it to one side, he tilted his head to look at her before looking away again. "And you will give me the answers I seek."

Retreating even further into the darker part of the cage, Artemis tracked him with her eye, silent as a shadow. Knowing it might be useless but still unwilling to just give up, Raphael started walking around the cage in hopes she would say something if he weren't looking at her directly. It was a difficult task, since his eyes seemed to go to her automatically, as though they were beyond his control. It was almost as if he feared she might disappear if he took his eyes off her for too long.

"Why are you killing my kind? Why come now, after so

many centuries have passed that your kind is simply a myth in this realm?" He looked at her from the corner of his eye before looking down at his shoes.

Still she said nothing. Raphael could feel her eyes on him like a caress, making all his senses hone in on her, yet she stayed silent.

"I see this will take time." His words were soft, almost as if he were speaking to himself, not to her. "But time is all I have, and I have plenty of it." Turning his head her way, he smiled sadly.

Raphael's words made Artemis's mind whirl with questions of her own. She knew she wouldn't voice them, but they gnawed at her, making her feel as though her stomach would empty itself where she stood. The loudest and most persistent one, that kept echoing in her head, *What is it about him that is so different from the rest of his kind?* bothered her the most. She shouldn't feel curiosity when it came to vampires. They had killed her mother and banished her kind. She only had hatred for them. Repeating it like a mantra, she silenced the questions and strengthened her resolve. She would bide her time and strike when he least expected it. When she killed him, all the issues that were making her doubt herself would be gone. With a slight tilt of her lips in a barely there smile she slowly sat down on the floor, and lifting up her knees, she leaned her arms on them. She can do this. She is stronger than all of them combined. Her smile grew as his frown appeared, pulling his eyebrows down on his handsome face.

"Somehow, that smile doesn't promise answers," he mused out loud, one side of his lips lifting slightly, and a soft, uncontrolled chuckle escaped her.

Raphael was going to say more, but a commotion outside the door made him turn his head sharply in that direction, and Artemis went on full alert. Confusion clouded her mind seeing him react almost as if he were protective of her, but that couldn't be true. Maybe he was worried about himself. If there was discord among the vampires, she knew she could use it to her advantage in getting out of here. With each passing moment the iron was draining out her strength, and regardless of how strong and stubborn she was, Artemis knew it wouldn't be long before she would be unable to run even if a chance presented itself. He opened his mouth as if to say something else, but the slamming of the door being flung open stopped him and made her spring upright in her prison.

"Ah! She's awake!" Claude walked in, all arrogant, glaring at her with disgust written plainly on his face.

"Why are you here?" Raphael glared back at him, knowing that any chance of getting Artemis to talk had been lost with Claude's dramatic entrance.

"Why? Did I interrupt something?" Claude snapped at him. "I can hear everything from across the place. It didn't seem like there was any conversation going on. Just you talking to yourself. And her killing more of us!"

Raphael searched Claude's face as hundreds of thoughts rattling in his head. This was beyond any obnoxious behavior he had ever seen or expected to see from his friend. Something very wrong was going on, and it bothered him to know that he would need to pull it out of both of them. Raphael knew he had to play this slow and smart if he was to get any answers, so straightening up, he smoothed his features and smiled at Claude.

"That idiot got what he deserved, and she is not much forthcoming, as you heard." He chuckled as if it were a joke between them. "Maybe my pretty face rendered her speechless, huh?" Smirking at Claude, he turned his head towards

Artemis and flinched internally at the wariness he saw in her good eye, focused solely on him.

"You have a point at that one being a waste of immortal life. And yeah, everyone does say you have the prettiest face. That's true." Relaxing his aggressive stance, Claude chuckled along with him "The ladies always had a weakness for it." A burst of laughter echoed around the garage.

"It's useless to keep trying now. Let's go and leave her to rethink her options." Walking up to Claude, Raphael slapped him on the back before turning him toward the door. "We'll come back later when she realizes that talking is her only hope of getting out of here alive." Winking at his friend, he pulled him out the door.

Reaching behind him, Raphael grabbed the door and pulled it closed. He didn't miss the hatred burning like a thousand suns in Artemis's eye, aimed directly at him, before he left.

Chapter Seventeen

She needed to get out of this place. Artemis knew this better than she'd known anything in her long life. The bloodsuckers were messing with her head, and she was feeling herself crumbling slowly. Three days. It had been three days that they've kept her in this iron cage. Raphael hasn't returned for longer than few blinks of an eye to ask his stupid questions, and when he didn't receive answers, he just sighed, rubbed the bridge of his nose and walked away. She had no intention of giving him any answers. She kept asking her own question, about where her arrow was, but all he would tell her was that it was safe. It would never be safe until it was in her hands, but she didn't tell him that. Her strength was slowly seeping out of her body and the injuries were not healing as fast as they usually would. This iron cage might very well be her tomb. Artemis was aware she needed to find a way to escape, but no opportunity had presented itself so far.

Sitting on the hard floor with her arms draped over her knees, she kept picking at the scab on her arm. It was courtesy of the iron bars, when she'd tried to pull them apart before falling unconscious for her efforts. She'd been lucky that no one had walked in, and Artemis now knew how stupid it was to do that when anyone could just walk in and drain her of her blood while in that state,. Not that they hadn't tried to take her blood. Twice a random vampire had stepped in when they thought she was sleeping, but it hadn't ended well for them. The blood staining everything around her, as well as her clothing, was the only evidence that those things had even existed before she got her hands on them. The iron weakened her, but she was still stronger than they were.

The creaking sound of the door opening alerted Artemis that she was no longer alone. Ignoring the noise, she kept picking at the scab while watching the form of whoever it was walk in from the corner of her eye. At first she thought it was Raphael coming again with his ridiculous questions. Her heart fluttered in her chest before stopping for a second. This one was leaner, not having so many firm muscles that she hated, because her eyes kept tracing them. That in itself got her to stiffen her shoulders, that whoever it was noticed, because a menacing chuckle sounded from the door.

"You know who the treat is, don't you, bug?" The condescending tone made Artemis turn her head slowly towards the vampire. "You don't stiffen like that when Raphael comes here." He laughed out loud at her glare.

She watched the bloodsucker—Claude was his name, from what she'd heard Raphael call him. With his hands clasped at his back, he walked around her cage, looking at his feet with occasional glances her way. He didn't say anything more, and she was quite happy to stay silent. It wasn't like she had anything to say to any of them anyway.

Claude's presence, however, was making her uneasy. After that first day when they'd brought her here, Artemis had not seen him—until now. She tracked his movement with her eyes.

"So let's try this my way, shall we?" Claude stopped few feet away from her prison, making her lips curve in an evil smirk while he glared at her.

"Come closer, why don't you? So we can try whatever it is that you want while we're face to face, huh?" Artemis's husky voice made Claude visibly shiver. Cocking her head at his reaction, her smirk grew. "You like it when I talk to you!"

"There is not one thing I like about you!" Claude snapped at her, his eyes turning amber and casting shadows around them. "Don't get lulled into a false sense of security here, bug! Raphael can't protect you from me. I am his king, and he will obey my orders!"

"Yet here I am, oh mighty king," she mocked him, while murder was written on his face at her words. "Alive and safe from all your orders. Why do you think that is?"

"We need to know what your people are planning. If you know what's good for you, you'll start talking. You have until sunrise. After that, I'll try my luck with the one that was with you when we pulled you here through the portal. I'm sure he'll be more than happy to talk." A sinister glint was in Claude's eyes as he watched for her reaction.

"He's still alive?" Artemis kept her voice sounding bored, hoping Claude would not notice that she was holding her breath, waiting for his answer.

"He's alive for now." She could almost hear his brain working behind his narrowed eyes. "Or maybe we're approaching this the wrong way. Maybe if I bring him here and drain him in front of you, you'll be more willing to talk." One of his perfect eyebrows lifted as if in question.

"He means nothing to me," Artemis chuckled, shaking her head "You know," she began. Lifting herself off the ground, she started pacing in front of him "I heard all these stories about you. The vampires, top of the food chain. I expected a lot more from you and your kind." Tsking at him, she made sure to display as much pity as she could manage. "Our younglings are stronger than you. When that portal opens, and have no doubt it will, it'll be a slaughter. I'll make sure to look for you when that time comes."

With a terrifying growl, Claude slammed his body into the bars of the cage, reaching his arm between them, trying to grab her. Twisting out of his way in a smooth motion, Artemis grabbed hold of his arm as she wrapped it around her own, making sure he couldn't escape. Yanking his head back by a handful of his long hair, she slammed it against the bars, making him hiss aa a crunching sound was heard when his nose broke. Everywhere the iron touched her skin was sizzling and hurting, but it was worth the pain when she saw blood dripping down his porcelain skin and covering his lips and chin. Just as she was planning to go for the kill, that alluring smell filled her lungs and she staggered back, releasing her hold on Claude.

"What the fuck is going on here?" Raphael was at Claude's side so fast that wind rustled Artemis's hair. "Claude? What were you thinking!!" he practically yelled in his king's face.

"What I was thinking?" Slamming both his hands into Raphael's chest, Claude sent him flying into the bars of the cage with such force that the cage slid a foot to the side. "What was I thinking?! This is a monster, Raphael!" he screamed in Raphael's face. "It's not a woman! It's not some poor suffering soul that needs saving or your fucking ticket to redemption of past sins! It's a fucking monster that will kill us all! And you're keeping her alive!"

"And she will stay alive until I have all the answers!" Raphael's voice surprised Artemis; it was deceptively calm. Too much so. "Go upstairs, Claude. Go play with your subjects, have your parties, orgies, whatever it is that you do. Stay away from this place until I'm done. If not..." Lifting himself up, Raphael tugged on his sleeves, straightening his suit jacket. "If not, I believe a battle may be overdue."

"After all these years, you would fight me for her?" Gaping in astonishment, Claude flings a hand in her direction.

Without a word, Raphael just watched him stoically. Confusion made Artemis lightheaded and she frowned, looking at the one vampire that she didn't have the urge to kill but hated more because of it. Why in all the worlds would he try to protect her? He is her jailer. The feel of his fingers on her face comes, uninvited, to her mind, and the pounding of her heart like a war drum got his attention. He didn't react, not really. Artemis was watching him so intently she couldn't help but notice the subtle stiffening of his shoulders, the barely perceptible tilt of his head towards her and most of all, the slight lift of the corners of his full lips. Claude's angry roar jolted her out of her fascinated observation.

"Until sunrise, Raphael! She has until sunrise to give you answers." Spittle flew from his mouth, and with his hair all mussed up, he looked like a wild animal. "After that, she's *mine*!!" With those last words, Claude left the garage so fast that the door banged twice, loudly, before falling from the frame and crashing to the ground. In the silence, the feminine giggle got Raphael's head snapping in her direction. Artemis was more surprised than anyone else.

Chapter Eighteen

What the hell was wrong with her? Artemis couldn't believe her own ears. She'd giggled! That hadn't happened since she was a youngling, and now here she was, laughing with her enemy while they're threatening her life. She must have had a horrified expression on her face, because Raphael tilted his head as his eyes softened and his lips curled up slightly. The expression on his face made butterflies dance inside her and feelings bubble up, tickling her throat. Her breathing deepened as she struggled to take a full breath. And while she had the internal struggle to not show weakness or reaction, he merely watched her. She could almost feel that pull towards him like a physical thing, making her drown in his green eyes. Fear gripped her that he might not need to kill her; she would sign her own death warrant by letting him drain her blood willingly if this continued.

"I will tell you nothing." Her voice was breathier than she liked, but at least the silence was broken.

Still watching her with that soft look in his eyes, he squinted a little before starting to take his jacket off. Artemis stiffened for a split second before her instincts took over and her knees bent slightly. She was ready to pounce in a blink of an eye. What made her frown was his deep sigh and the shake of his head at her reaction. Before she could process the absurdity of the situation, he folded the jacket in half and dropped it next to the cage. Without giving her time to react, Raphael turned his back on her and sat down, leaning back against the bars.

Artemis couldn't do anything but stare at the back of his head. In his right mind, the bloodsucker had not just turned his back on her but had made sure she could rip his head off if she wanted to! Her heart picked up a beat and she clenched her hands in tight fists while almost panting, like she had fought an army. It must be some game, some trick.

"Either try to kill me or sit down so we can talk." Raphael rubbed his hands over his face while his deep voice wreaked chaos in her. He sounded exhausted.

Wary of his agenda and of everything else that happened in the last hour, Artemis walked away from him and sat down away from the iron bars, staring intently at the back of his head. The black shirt he was wearing was stretched out, hugging his shoulders, while her fingers twitched to reach out and touch him. She clutched her knees to her chest so she wouldn't do anything stupid as she watched Raphael roll up his sleeves up to his forearms, his biceps bunching the fabric and luring her eyes.

"I'm not sure there is anything to talk about," she told him, absently, and he stopped his movement when she spoke.

"No creature decides to go on a killing spree without a reason unless it's gone insane. I should know that, since I've done it." After he finished rolling up his other sleeve, Raphael leaned his head back on the bars. "And since you are very clearly sane, I need to know what brought this about."

"You sound very certain of my state of mind." Artemis snorted at his words. "What makes you think I'm sane?"

"Good point." Raphael chuckled turning his head so she could see his profile "Sanity is a relative term, isn't it?"

"What is it that you want from me?" He stopped his chuckling as she spoke. "I will not tell you anything that will harm my people. You must know this."

Quietly he replied, "Is that what you think I'm trying to do? Harm your people?" Artemis could see his forehead bunching up in a frown in profile "Do I need to remind you that you came here after the devil only knows how many centuries? You came to us and started killing." Taking a deep breath, Raphael shook his head.

"Some debts need to be paid, bloodsucker!" Artemis hissed at him. "Some debts are not forgotten, no matter how much time it takes to collect!"

"And that is exactly what I need to know." His words were so quiet she could barely hear him. "Who has done what to unleash this hell upon us?"

"You think this is hell?" Artemis snickered. "They were just at the wrong place at the right time." Tilting her head, she watched him stiffen. "I was simply curious and played with them a little."

"Taking a life is a game to you?"

"If said life has debts to pay?" Artemis sobered up at his words. "Yes!"

"What is this debt that you think we owe? Don't you want to talk first and see what can be done before an all-out war starts? Innocent humans will die in the process. Do your people have so little regard towards life?"

"I don't want to talk nor do I care if all humans die!" Jumping up, Artemis glared at him. "I want revenge!"

At her outburst, Raphael froze. They were still like statues for long moments, his mind swirling with a million thoughts at once as she glared at him.

"Revenge for what?" Pushing himself off the ground, Raphael slowly turned to face her. His green eyes sparkled in the lighting, making them seem like glass orbs. "Who is the one that wronged you so that you seek revenge?"

Artemis watched him and all her fight drained out of her. He appeared calm, but that was only a mask. At her words, the temperature in the place had dropped by a few degrees and his chiseled body seemed like almost to have turned into marble. His beautiful face was shaded with shadows that danced off of his high cheekbones and perfect aquiline nose. His full lips were pressed firmly together and a muscle was ticking in his jaw.

Unaware of what she was doing, Artemis slowly walked towards him. The way he was standing and the energy coming off of him was telling her he was more upset on her behalf than interested to hear who would die next and for what. Without thinking, she lifted her hand, and reaching between the bars, she cupped his face. Closing his eyes, Raphael nuzzled her hand as if it were the most natural thing in the world. Her stomach clenched at the touch and her heart sped up, making it difficult to breathe. At the quickening beat, his eyes snapped open, looking straight at her.

"Revenge for what?" He repeated his question, placing his hand over hers and trapping her there.

"My mother." Her nostrils flared as she struggled with so many conflicting emotions that everything around her started to spin. "Your people and the humans killed my mother." It was difficult to breathe, and Artemis was grateful he had hold of her hand. It was the only thing keeping her standing.

Raphael cursed out loud, closing his eyes tightly as if her words pained him. She wondered why in the world he would even care about her mother. When louder cursing came from him, she sluggishly lifted her eyelids, unaware she'd had them closed. Everything was spinning around, out of control, and she groaned, pressing her lips together tightly so she didn't spill the contents of her stomach over them both.

One second Raphael held her hand pressed to his face across the iron bars. The next, metal groaned and there were sounds of crashing before her world turned upside down. She started to wonder if this was her end. It sure felt like it. The next second, she felt like she was freefalling before her body was cradled to a firm chest. Her face was nestled between a shoulder and neck where that scent she found herself addicted to was so intense she almost cried in fear. Was he going to poison her?

"I've got you," Raphael mumbled in her hair. "Just don't fucking die! I've got you."

Holding Artemis pressed to his chest and in a panic that he'd never known before, Raphael left Claude's manor behind him. He was sure with the speed he was going that no one knew they left, not even Claude. There would be hell to pay for this, but he couldn't let anything happen to her. He might die for his stupidity, but there was no turning back. This would either help, and she would know he meant her no harm, or she would kill him and destroy this entire realm. Still cursing in every language he knew, cradling her like the most precious thing in his life, Raphael disappeared into the darkness.

Chapter Nineteen

"Why on earth did you think it was a smart idea to come to my door?!" Iris glared at Raphael as he shouldered his way past her to enter her shop. "Come right in, why doncha?" she yelled at his back.

Raphael ignored the witch as he stormed through the store and headed straight for the room at the back where all the statues were. It was the only place that came to mind as he saw Artemis's eyes roll to the back of her head and she collapsed. Fear that it might be too late to do anything for her gripped him like a vise, and he couldn't take a full breath. With Iris following behind him cursing gods, vampires and the Fae alike, Raphael kicked open the doors of the room and walked right to the middle of it.

Laying the Fae gently on the floor, he pushed the stray strands that had escaped her braid away from her face. Artemis looked pale and she was still unresponsive. If it weren't for her barely audible heartbeat, Raphael would've thought she'd died.

"Can the iron kill her?" he asked Iris, not looking away from the woman in front of him.

"What's wrong with her? I thought you wanted her dead." Iris walked towards him slowing her steps and frowning when she saw him gently cradling Artemis's face in his palm. "What changed in three days, vampire?" she hissed at him.

"Can the iron kill her?" There was a warning in the words that passed Raphael's clenched teeth, although his hands stayed gentle on Artemis.

"No!" Iris huffed incredulously at him. "It weakens her, but it won't kill her. Did you fight? Is that way she's covered in dried blood?" Scrunching up her nose, she peered over his shoulder at Artemis.

"Do something, then, witch!" Turning his head to glare at her, Raphael gestured with his free hand toward Artemis's body. "She was talking one minute, then she collapsed. Wake her up!"

"Do I look like a doctor to you?" Placing her hands on her hips, Iris glared at the damn arrogant man.

"Do not test me this moment, Iris! My control is holding by a thread, and I can't promise your safety. Do something to wake her up." Looking at her eyes, he let the panic he felt show and Iris's green eyes widened at that. "I know you can help her. You took her companion with you for that reason. You asked for my help and I gave it without questioning your motives. I'm asking you to do the same now." Swallowing hard as if unfamiliar with the words, he whispered "Please."

Iris looked at him for a long moment before he saw in her eyes the moment she reached some sort of a decision. Her magic crackled and pushed at his chest the same way as always, but he now understood that it was not threatening him, it was merely how it worked. Pressing her lips in a firm line, nostrils flaring, she gave him a firm nod before turning around and bolting out of the room. His chest contracted in worry as he watched her black hair fly behind her just as her long dress bellowed and her bare feet slapped a fast rhythm on the floors.

"Iris will help you get better. I know she can." Raphael mumbled to Artemis as he looked back down at her. "And when you open your eyes, you will tell me everything so that I can fix this…Whatever this is that's going on."

She didn't reply. Of course, she wouldn't. Her skin was getting paler by the minute and her body was getting colder. Without overthinking his reaction, Raphael ripped his shirt open and lifted her up so she could lean her upper body on him. The corset she was wearing left enough exposed skin to assure him there would be enough skin contact. After holding her like that for a couple of minutes and not noticing a difference, he ripped her corset off with a flick of his wrist and pressed her more firmly to him. Something snapped inside him like a rubber band under too much tension with her breasts pressed to his chest and her face nestled in the crook of his neck. With a strong force, warmth burst from the center of his chest and entered Artemis. She gasped for air like she hadn't been breathing a second before her eyes snapped open and locked on his. The same heat exited her chest and hit him like a battering ram, almost making him drop her. As he gasped for air as well, she went limp in his arms again.

"Okay, I think I got it right!" Iris was rushing to his side, stopping Raphael from overthinking what happened. "You need to place her down, vampire."

Iris reached for Artemis so she could pull her away from him. Raphael hissed at her like a demon possessed, making

Iris stumble backward few steps with eyes as wide as dinner plates. Tightening his arms around Artemis, he bared his fangs at Iris, making her tremble visibly where she stood.

"I'm not going to hurt her!" Slowly lifting both her hands in surrender, Iris spoke softly as if speaking to a scared child. "You asked me to help her, remember? She's still unresponsive." She waved her hand, indicating Artemis, whose head was lolling to the side. "I must touch her to be able to help her." She waited to see if she'd gotten through to him.

"Give me a moment, witch. I don't know what happened." Raphael shook his head as if to clear it, but he still didn't loosen up his hold on Artemis.

"Take your time, I'm not planning on moving until you're back to your annoying, arrogant self," Iris assured him with so much sincerity in her voice that it almost made him laugh.

"You're either fearless, witch, or, you're stupid." Shaking his head, he chuckled a little and his arms loosened their death grip on Artemis.

"I'll go with number two!" she chirped with a grimace on her pretty face. "I must be stupid to agree to deal with a vampire in the first place."

"Help her. I think she's suffering, I just don't know from what." Shielding Artemis with his body, Raphael took his shirt off and covered her before sliding away from her enough that Iris could approach her. He was still sitting close enough that his leg was touching her body.

Picking up the things she'd dropped, Iris knelt next to Artemis. Lifting her head slightly, the witch opened a bottle and started pouring the water into the Fae's mouth. Raphael frowned. It took a moment before Artemis poked out her tongue, licking the droplets from her lips before she latched on to the bottle like an infant. The water was gone in a second.

"Just as I thought." Iris glanced at Raphael from the corner of her eye. "You forgot that she's not a vampire. No water and I guess, no food either, for three days?" She kept her voice conversational, not wanting to provoke him.

"Fuck!" Raphael snapped, making Iris jump a little as he stood up and started pacing while gripping his hair in both hands. "Fuck, fuck, fuck!!!"

"You didn't think of it."

"The fuck you mean I didn't *think* of it? I fucking starved her almost to death!" he roared in her face, making her flinch.

"It happens." Iris spoke softly, trying to placate him. "How often do you keep a Fae caged?"

"I would take a wild guess and say not often." Artemis's softly spoken words made both Iris and Raphael freeze. The next second, Raphael was kneeling next to her head with his palm cupping her face.

"Are you okay?" he searched her eyes.

"I've been better." She tried to smile at him, but she wasn't successful. *Why in the worlds do I want to smile at him?* her mind screamed before realization hit her out of nowhere that she was feeling emotions that weren't her own.

"What happened, apart from you being dehydrated and starved?" Iris asked Artemis as she opened another bottle and handed it over. "Sip it slowly, or it'll make you sick," she pointed out.

"Something I never thought would happen to me in a million years. Not in the middle of my enemies." Artemis spoke, lost in thought while clutching the bottle in her hand and looking at Iris as if the other woman were her lifeline. Iris frowned, not understanding what was going on.

Venus Trap

Raphael held his breath. As long as she was breathing, he was sure he could fix whatever had happened at Claude's home that he didn't know about. He watched intently, preparing himself to hear some horrible news. Artemis looked at Iris without blinking for what felt like an eternity. Wetting her lips, she swallowed audibly before taking a sip of water and clearing her throat.

"I found my mate…" Artemis said, still looking at Iris.

Raphael frowned before anger bubbled in his chest like never before. He was a second from bolting out of the witch's place to storm Claude's manor, intending to kill them all. Then slowly Artemis's eyes locked on his. In his feral state, it took him a moment to realize the weight of her words. Coming back to himself, he realized he had his fangs out and was hunched over on all fours, hissing at them both. His muscles were bunched up and he was coiled for an attack. Warmth washed over him at that look in her eyes, and he slumped on the floor as his fangs retreated. A wolfish grin split his lips, and he sheepishly shrugged his shoulder at Iris, who rolled her eyes at him.

"Good luck with this one." Iris told Artemis somberly. "He's as arrogant and stubborn as they come."

Raphael's grin only grew as he kept looking at Artemis so intently that she felt her insides burning. She watched him warily, but there was a glint in her eyes that he didn't miss.

Chapter Twenty

Artemis nibbled on an apple as she watched Raphael pace back and forward in the small room that Iris had given her. Confusion, more than the lack of food and water, was making her lightheaded. She could easily have blamed it on the male in the room with her, but she was aware that she hadn't even thought of eating or drinking for herself. She was so intent on staying alive, learning something that could give her an advantage or find a way to escape that she never once thought of water or food.

"I'll check the perimeter from the outside. I'll be right back." Raphael's words brought her out of her head. "You'll stay here!" he told her firmly, and her lips twitched at the stern look on his handsome face.

"Or what?" Tilting her head, she watched him stiffen. That scent that was driving her crazy and she had thought was poison started making a lot of sense right now. "Are you going to kill me, Raphael?" Her smile grew as a growl rumbled in his chest.

Raphael shivered and almost went to ravish her at the sound of his name on her lush lips. It did stupid things to him like he wasn't centuries old, but rather a teenager with a hormonal imbalance. The worst part was that she knew what she was doing to him and enjoyed every damn minute, by the looks of it.

"I need to know that Claude is nowhere near this place." Walking towards her, he sat next to her on the small sofa, feeling like she was almost in his lap. "I want you to rest for the time being, because in my desire to find out what was going on, I neglected you completely. Something is going on and I will get to the bottom of it, I assure you. Claude knows something, because that was not usual behavior, even for him."

Artemis searched his eyes, mutely weighing his words. It was such a peculiar feeling to be aware when someone was telling the truth. She wasn't aware of what had happened from the time she lost consciousness to the time she opened her eyes at that ritual room in Iris's shop. Whatever it was, it had bonded her to Raphael, and now she knew that she could never hurt him. Well, not physically, at least. She was still unsure if she would stick around long enough to discover how they had bonded. It wasn't a full bond, but it was the beginning of one. She'd only heard stories about it. The pull and compulsion to complete it was a living thing that she fought with everything in her. Lazarus would definitely lose his shit when he finds out. She groaned internally at that thought.

"Are you listening to me?" Raphael cupped her face, his thumb rubbing her cheekbone gently, bringing her to the present. "Stop plotting for a second...please." That last word sounded pained as if it hurt him to say it. "We will figure this out together, I promise." He searched her face. "I can't believe I'm going to say this, but... I will help you revenge your mother's death. No matter who it was that was responsible for it. You have my word."

"Why would you do that?" Artemis narrowed her eyes. "Mate or not, this is not your fight. Although it is your war...on the opposite side of mine, need I remind you." Still unable to remove his hand because for some ridiculous reason it felt good when he was touching her, she glared at him. "How do you know that you are not one of those that killed her? Do you remember every life you've taken over the centuries?"

"I can assure you I was not part of whatever happened when your mother was killed." Truth rang clear in his words, making her bristle.

"How can you be sure? You're a predator just like me! A killer!" her voice rose with each word. His sad smile deflated her like a balloon. She frowned at that look on his face.

"I've only killed one woman in my entire existence." Raphael's words made her eyebrows hit her hairline. She looked at him incredulously. "And I assure you, she was not your mother. Nor was she a Fae of any kind."

Coldness surrounded her at his words and shadows were evident in his eyes from whatever demons were haunting him still. Artemis felt an irresistible urge to embrace him; make him forget whatever it was that clouded his eyes, but she gripped the blanket covering her with tight fists just to keep her hands to herself. As if reading her mind, Raphael pried her fingers open and laced his calloused fingers through hers. His other hand went back to cupping her face again, and his eyes held her captive. He didn't need an iron cage to keep her a prisoner. Those green eyes of his, like ancient forests from her home, were so intense that Artemis felt like they were reaching inside her soul and would hold her captive for eternity. She knew it as well as she knew her name. And he was telling the truth. This was very, very bad. She needed time to think.

"I don't think I can move from this spot if I tried. Your prisoner will await her jailer right where he leaves her."

"You are not my prisoner anymore, Artemis." Raphael told her gently, making goosebumps cover her arms and legs. "Not anymore. I would like to think we can get past the last few days and start fresh. As a team."

"You cannot pet something that you've held in a cage and ask it to love you."

Raphael's body jerked at her words like she had slapped him. Artemis watched so many feelings flick through his eyes that she felt sick to her stomach for saying those words to him. When such deep sadness and loneliness stayed, plain as a bright sunny day for her to see, her cold heart shattered into thousand pieces for him. That one moment of vulnerability showed her that the two of them might not be so different after all. She was preparing herself to reach up and touch him voluntarily when he abruptly stood up. She missed his touch the second it was gone. The blood in her veins turned cold from the hurt visible on his face.

"I deserved that." Raphael told her, looking down at her. "But before you judge me too harshly, tell me one thing. What would you have done if the roles were reversed? If it was me coming to your realm, killing the people you call friends?"

"I have no friends." Her words were out before she could stop them. He looked at her without any expression on his face for a long moment.

"After tonight," Raphael turned his head to look out the window, seemingly lost in thought, "neither have I, it seems." Artemis swallowed the lump in her throat at his softly spoken words. "I'll be back."

With those words, he left the room, his incredible speed making a cup topple off the table and the curtains sway in the breeze that formed. Artemis kept looking at the slightly opened door he left in his wake.

Chapter Twenty-One

It's been a very long time since Raphael had felt so torn up inside. Immortality was something humans went to great lengths to achieve, not understanding the burden of it—how you lose yourself and become numb to everything as the years go by. He'd been sure of that... until he met Artemis.

He was numb.

In three days, she managed to turn his entire existence inside out. There were so many feelings inside him that he felt like his skin was stretching to accommodate them all, and he half-expected to burst into thousand pieces at any moment. She called him a mate. His heart thumped loudly in his chest at that thought.

A mate!

After being alone for so long, those words made him feel alive for the first time in centuries. He was ready to rip the worlds and realms apart to keep her at his side. Anissa didn't take this from him to her death. Then Artemis said those words that cut him more deeply than any he has ever heard. *You cannot pet something you hold in a cage and ask it to love you.* Her words echoed in his head like she was standing next to him, repeating them over and over again. They didn't change how he felt or the lengths he was prepared to go for her. They just left a wound that would bleed forever. Every time he looked at her.

As he walked amongst the shadows of the night, hiding his presence even though the city looked deserted at this hour, Raphael felt restless. He was itching to go back to her. In case she decided to run, he told himself. A smile tugged at his lips at that thought. He would love to chase her, his instincts went into high gear at the idea. But first he had to hear the full story. To know what made her come here now. Why wait so long? Or were they coming and going with no one the wiser about their presence? Was her mother killed recently? Too many questions, not enough answers, he decided as he made a full circle around the store, jumping from roof to roof.

Dropping silently into a crouch, Raphael straightened, ready to walk back inside, when he felt the power radiating at his back. His back stiffened as he slowly turned around, concealing how uneasy it made him feel, and settled his eyes on Claude.

"It didn't take you long to track me down." Placing his hands in his pockets, Raphael nonchalantly faced his friend. *Or is he a friend?* The question rattled around in his head. "So what do we do now, Claude?"

"Where is she?" The coldness in Claude's voice brought every protective instinct Raphael had to the front.

"She is with me," he answered, keeping a tight rein on his control so as not to give away anything. "That's all you need to know."

"I would have to disagree on that count…old friend."

Glaring, Claude took a step closer, making Raphael pull his hands out of his pockets. "I'll ask again. Where is she?" He took another slow step, now standing half in the shadows and half in the yellowish glow of a street light not far from them. "Don't make me send them to look for her while I keep you busy."

"You have grown too complacent, Claude, if you think you and a handful of useless immortal lives can keep me busy. Or that I will let any of you to walk past me." Shaking his head, Raphael chuckled humorlessly.

He watched the shadows move from the corner of his eye and counted seven in total. They stayed in the shadows as if that would save their pathetic lives. He has been away for too long, Raphael decided. The idiots believe they can take him. It was almost insulting.

"She is a monster, Raphael!" Claude hissed at him, baring his fangs as his eyes turned amber, glowing in the darkness. "She is hunting and killing our kind, and here you are protecting her!" The last words were almost roared in his face. A dog barked somewhere in the distance.

"The question is not why I'm protecting her." Raphael spoke calmly even when his entire body was poised for attacking. "The question here...old friend...is what and who are you protecting?"

Raphael didn't expect to see the surprise so plainly visible on Claude's face. The widening of his eyes as he took a barely perceptible step back was almost comical. So he wasn't expecting to be called out on it. *How interesting,* Raphael thought to himself. Either Claude thought himself very astute and subtle, or he thought Raphael was an idiot. There was no other explanation for his reaction.

"She's messing with your head." Claude sounded defensive, instead of his normal aloof self. "Or the madness has finally gotten to you from living alone for so long." He tried to act concerned, making Raphael grind his teeth.

"What are you hiding, Claude?" With a sigh, Raphael moved his head from side to side, cracking his neck. "This is the last time I'm going to ask." He lifted a hand to stop the words that were going to come out of Claude's mouth. "It may also be your last chance to answer it, too, so choose your words wisely." Raphael waved his palm around, encompassing the seven still lurking in the shadows. "They seem agitated and restless."

After long moments Claude spoke, and he deflated in front of Raphael's eyes, confusing the hell out of him. "You don't know what you're getting yourself into here, Raphael. Some things should be left buried."

"Well, I was kinda dragged into this by a friend." He narrowed his eyes at Claude, not trusting him for a second. "No one asked me what I wanted until all your shit came out to stink up my life. So speak. I wasn't joking! This is your last chance."

As Claude opened his mouth to say something, the seven lurking vampires decided that they had waited long enough and took matters into their own hands. All seven came at Raphael at once. Claude closed his half-open mouth as he watched them surround Raphael. *Raphael is right. They really are useless immortal lives,* he thought to himself as he shook his head.

He stood with his arms crossed and watched Raphael spring into action. One second he was standing calmly but alert. The next he was a whirlwind of movement no mortal eyes could follow. Claude's eyes widened as he saw Raphael twist and turn, his body a work of art, using the men and women around him against each other without getting caught in the middle. Either Raphael had been training while he was hiding from the world or something else was going on. It almost seemed as if he was faster and stronger than anything Claude had ever seen in his life.

Three men were ripped apart just as Claude finished his thought. Raphael wasn't slowing, he was getting invigorated and becoming faster. Before Claude could process that thought, there was only one of their kind left standing in front of Raphael with a horrified look on her face. Locking eyes with Claude, Raphael smiled before he grabbed both her arms and his foot connected with her chest as he kicked out. A gut-wrenching crunching sound was heard as her ribcage shattered, collapsing her lungs and heart before both her arms were ripped off. Still not taking his eyes off Claude, Raphael threw them to the side and his smile grew. Claude couldn't remember the last time he'd felt fear like he did at this moment.

"Last chance, Claude." Raphael said softly. "And I must say, that was fun." He wasn't even breathing hard and dread pooled in Claude's stomach. "It's been too long."

"Let's go inside to talk." Claude swallowed the lump in his throat. "Even the walls have ears."

After watching him for few more seconds through narrowed eyes, Raphael gave him a sharp nod. Turning around, he strode towards the shop where Iris already held the door open, not blinking an eye at the massacre Raphael had left in the middle of the street. *This is like a nightmare coming to life*, Claude thought as his feet started moving slowly to follow Raphael. He waved his hand behind him, indicating that someone needed to clean the mess up before any humans saw it. He felt the answering pull from those he had told to stay behind that it would be done. They turned to ashes eventually, but by the time that happened it would be too late to keep themselves a secret. Claude watched Iris as he entered the shop for any reaction, but the witch just gave him a tight smile.

"As long as I'm on the winning side, he can kill whoever he wants," she told him, as if reading his mind.

Claude's eyes connected with violet ones as soon as the door closed behind him. His steps faltered and he stopped, as if some invisible force held him captive.

"'I was hoping you would be stupid enough to attack him," Artemis said, conversationally leaning on the doorframe as if she could barely stand. "I was so ready to come and play, oh mighty king." She smirked at him as Claude watched, dumbfounded, as Raphael rushed to her side and picked her up, cradling her to his chest.

Artemis wrapped her arms around Raphael's neck and looked at Claude over his shoulder. Claude's mouth opened and closed a few times without anything coming out of it. He felt an arm wind through his and he flinched like a mortal at the contact, making Iris smile at him knowingly. He allowed her to pull him further inside the store.

Chapter Twenty-Two

Artemis ignored Claude as if he were not even present in the room. She watched Raphael as he placed her gently on the sofa and tucked the blanket around her as though she were a fragile thing that might break. He still wouldn't look at her, even when he was fussing about her as if she were a child. She gripped the blanket with both hands to stop herself from reaching out and touching him.

"Let's hear it, Claude. There's no time like the present," Raphael said, not turning around to look at his king.

"Maybe I should leave..." Iris's words trailed off when Raphael looked at her sharply. "Or I'll just sit right here. It's not like I have anything else to do," she finished lamely, plopping down on a chair close to Artemis.

"I'm not sure how smart it is to open old wounds." Claude looked at Raphael warily. "Some things are left unspoken so they can be forgotten. When you start poking, you might wish you had left it alone."

"Little late for that now, isn't it?" Lifting an eyebrow, Raphael sat on the edge of the sofa as if he couldn't bring himself to be away from Artemis. "When people start dying, I think it's time we start poking."

"I don't know anything for a fact, I must warn you," Claude started, and Raphael narrowed his eyes at the same second. "Don't look at me like that! This was long before our time, and I only know about it because unlike you, I never resisted our maker," he finished angrily.

Without interrupting him, Raphael waved his hand for Claude to continue. Noticing how Artemis tensed at Claude's words, he reached for her hand and laced their fingers together, giving her hand a reassuring squeeze. Claude watched the whole thing with a shocked expression on his face.

"This is bad." Claude shook his head. "Very bad!"

"You're not here to give relationship advice. Keep talking!" Raphael growled, as his eyes flashed amber, making Claude swallow thickly.

"As I said. From what I remember, the Fae were present in this world as much as we were. Anissa used to talk about them all the time. The story she told was that they had a queen who ruled both the dark and the light Fae and was well loved by her people." Claude's eyes flicked to Artemis, who was watching him intently. "I remember hearing a lot about how mesmerizing her violet eyes were."

Artemis's breathing grew heavy, and she was almost panting while she focused on Claude with laser precision. Raphael, not wanting to interrupt Claude since he wanted to finally understand what was going on and what he was dealing with, pulled Artemis into his lap, wrapping his arms around her and startling her. Tucking her under his chin like it was the most natural thing in the world, he kissed the top of her head, confusing the hell out of her, and he looked expectantly at Claude.

"Not many details were shared about what happened, exactly, but, Anissa liked to brag how the Queen's consort had a weakness for her and was visiting her often. Behind the Queen's back, he professed his love for our maker and convinced Anissa to help him take over the throne."

"What was his name?" Raphael asked out of nowhere, as if reading Artemis's mind.

"The consort?" Claude frowned "Lazarus, I believe."

"How?" The question came from Artemis as she straightened in Raphael's lap, glaring at Claude. "Help him take the throne how?"

Claude set ramrod straight, only his eyes moving from Artemis to Raphael and back. The tension grew by the second and soon became so thick it could almost be cut with a knife.

"By helping him kill the queen." Claude's voice was utterly emotionless, as if he was simply stating a fact.

"You lie!!" Artemis screamed, jumping at him so fast and away from Raphael that he almost missed grabbing her to hold her back.

"I'm only telling you what I know!" Claude roared, jumping up himself to get out of her reach. "Isn't that what you wanted?" He stared accusingly at Raphael.

"Let him tell his story, please." Raphael looked at Artemis. "It'll be more than what we have to go on now. I can't help you if I don't know anything."

"He's lying!" Artemis still glared at Claude even when she swayed, and only Raphael's hold on her arm stopped her from collapsing on the floor. "He's trying to stay alive by placing the blame on others for what the vampires and humans did!"

"He's a vampire, too!" Claude snapped at her, stabbing a finger at Raphael.

"Let him finish talking, Artemis. Let's hear it out. It can't hurt to hear the same story from both sides." Raphael tried to calm her down. Artemis nodded jerkily but refused to sit back down, still glaring at Claude.

"I don't know any details of how they did whatever it was that they did to kill her. I just know that before she died, she cursed the portal." With a sigh, Claude rubbed his face with his hands. "It closed and trapped the Fae on the other side. Anissa tried anything and everything to get it to open, but no luck. She took it out on all of us when another attempt failed. Many lost their lives at her hand for failing to open that damn portal."

"Cursed it how?" Artemis asked barely above a whisper while dread pooled in her stomach. She knew her mother's greatest power as well as weapon had been manifesting anything she wanted with the sound of her voice and spoken words.

"No one but her blood can be called from one realm to the other. Nothing but ancient magic can find the first secret. No one but a warrior with a bleeding heart can take the Obsidian throne. Until then, the realms will never merge." Everything came out in a rush, all in one breath as if Claude had been rehearsing it.

With a gasp, Artemis's body jerked back as if he'd slapped her and she plopped on the sofa before jumping right back up. Wide-eyed, she looked from Claude to Raphael and back. Her breathing sped up and her pupils dilated, almost hiding the color of her eyes. Raphael reached for her, but she batted his arms away.

"You're lying," she whispered.

"I have nothing to gain or lose at this point, bug. I have no reason to lie to you." Claude glared at her.

"Next time you call her a bug, I will rip your tongue out,

Claude," Raphael snapped, taking a step towards him, releasing Artemis. "At least I won't have to listen to you speak until it grows back!"

"Raphael…" Artemis called his name weakly, but before he could react, she dropped to the floor in a heap.

Scooping her up, Raphael called to Iris, "Get water, witch!"

Chapter Twenty-Three

Iris was frozen in her seat from what she heard when Raphael's words snapped her out of her shock. Jumping up from her chair, she ran toward the little kitchen to grab water and towels. Her mind spinning, she worked methodically on autopilot. *Only ancient magic can find the first secret.* Claude's words were circling in her head.

"Now, witch!" Raphael's bellow spurred her on, and she ran back.

Falling on her knees next to the sofa, Iris started squeezing the water from the towel and pressing it to Artemis's face and neck. Her hands trembled while she pushed energy from her body into Artemis and she was acutely aware of the two vampires looming over her.

"What's happening to her?" If Iris hadn't been scared of being ripped to pieces if something happened to Artemis, she would've laughed at the panic in Raphael's voice. "Why is her body flicking like that?!"

"I think someone is trying to pull her back through the

portal..." Iris mumbled with a frown. "It feels like she's fighting it; trying to stay here."

"Maybe it's for the better..."

"If I hear one more word from you, Claude, until she opens her eyes, you will regret the day we met." Raphael cut him off through clenched teeth. "Witch, I know you can do something, so do it now. I don't give a fuck about your secrets, and I'll be in your debt if you help me."

Looking over her shoulder at him, Iris weighed her options. She'd been hiding from the world all her life in fear of this exact thing. It was too late now to hide, after helping to pull Artemis here. She could help and hope that she picked the right side for good, or she could pretend she can't and end up dead. Raphael was getting crazier by the second; his eyes glowing amber and his fangs gleaming in the light, closer to her neck than she would've liked. Sending a quick prayer to her ancestors, Iris hoped she was making the right decision.

"Place your hand over her heart. Your bond started forming, so I'll use you as an anchor." She waved at Raphael, who had his hand in position before she finished talking while Claude gasped at the revelation. "I just hope she doesn't kill me for doing this," Iris finished under her breath.

Covering Raphael's hand over Artemis's chest and ignoring Claude's mutterings, Iris started humming. Barely audible at first but getting louder by the moment. Raphael kept flicking his eyes from Artemis's face to the witch's fingers on her free hand. She was doing that finger to finger touching again, and if he hadn't been out of his mind about possibly losing Artemis, his curiosity would've pushed him to grill her for answers.

Something was cooling inside Raphael's chest. He couldn't quite name the feeling, but it was like a door had been opened in his chest and a blizzard was pushing in full force. In all his years, he'd never felt anything like it. He wasn't worried that something was happening to him; the panic he felt was because he was sure that was how Artemis felt inside at the moment. His lungs shrunk from it and he couldn't take a full breath. As the humming grew in volume, the chill started gradually fading, being replaced with a warm breeze slowly filling the center of his chest. His hand pressing on Artemis's chest was getting uncomfortably warm.

"You better not hurt her!" he growled at Iris, but the witch ignored him like he was a harmless human.

For the umpteenth time since he met her, Raphael wandered if Iris was so powerful that she didn't fear him, no matter how inconspicuous she was trying to be. Or else she was stupid. There was no other explanation. If he had to bet, he would bet on the first. No one is that stupid when they have inch-long fangs a hairsbreadth from their neck. Aware that his mind was thinking ridiculous thoughts just to keep him from going berserk, Raphael kept looking intently at Artemis.

"You know this can't happen, right?" Claude brought him out of his head and Raphael gave him a death glare. "You can glare at me as much as you want, but this," Claude waved a hand between Raphael and Artemis. "Whatever this is, it's a disaster waiting to happen, and it'll get us all killed. Anissa's messing with the Fae is biting us in the ass now, centuries later. You want to follow her lead?" He lifted an eyebrow, daring Raphael to argue.

"I didn't ask you for an opinion or advice." Raphael dismissed him, turning his head towards Artemis as her eyes fluttered open, making him take his first full breath since she collapsed on the floor.

"It's what they do, Raphael! They fuck with our minds, getting us obsessed with them so they can use us as pawns and manipulate us. Are you fucking blind?!"

Raphael didn't take his eyes off Artemis as she opened her eyes and finally focused on him. When her lips quirked at the corners, he gave her a sheepish smile and cupped her face, rubbing his thumb over her bottom lip. Not even Iris snorting at him could lessen the relief he felt to see Artemis here with him completely. He searched her eyes and saw when they softened at his worry.

"I'm well now. I don't feel pulled anymore." Artemis's husky voice gave Raphael goosebumps all over.

"Are you sure? Can it happen again without us being aware?" He didn't care that everyone in that room could hear that this woman had became his biggest weakness. Let them try to take her away from him.

"No. I felt the pull too late earlier. The way they pulled me from the other side felt like my body was being pried open from the inside out in the middle of winter. Now that I know what to look for, I'll stay aware," she told him somberly.

As soon as she finished talking, Raphael smiled at her. Her smile stayed frozen in place, because as soon as she blinked, Raphael was gone and he had Claude pinned to the wall by his neck, his feet a foot off the floor. Plaster was raining down on them both and there was a Claude-sized hole in the wall. Iris was groaning painfully next to Artemis, hiding her face in her hands and looking pitiful. Artemis didn't know when things had changed and she had started caring about people, but it bothered her that Raphael was upset and that Iris was unhappy. The mate bond explained why she felt that way about Raphael, and feeling Iris's energy helping her fight the pull that she had no doubt Lazarus was doing made her look at the witch with new eyes. She didn't want to overthink it or contemplate how stupid and dangerous that was. At the moment she had way too many questions, and Raphael was trying to kill the only source she had for answers.

"Raphael, let him go." She had no strength to speak out loud, but he heard her and his head turned in her direction that same second. "Please. He has information we need if what he says is true."

"I'll say it again. I have nothing to gain by lying," Claude rasped while trying to claw at Raphael's hand that was wrapped like a noose around his neck.

Ignoring Claude like he wasn't even there, Artemis didn't look away from Raphael. "Please," she repeated, reaching out her hand towards him.

Raphael was by her side before she blinked while Claude dropped to the floor coughing, with more plaster raining down on him as Iris giggled before slapping a hand over her mouth.

Chapter Twenty-Four

"This is insane!" Still coughing, Claude lifted himself off the floor, dusting off his clothing and making clouds of dust around him.

"You're absolutely sure that the name was Lazarus?" Artemis ignored his mutterings and got right to the point." And he killed the queen?"

"If Anissa lied to me, I'm lying to you. I said it's what I was told, not that it was a fact." Affronted, Claude glared at her.

"That's your maker?" Tilting her head, she studied his reaction while feeling Raphael stiffen next to her.

Iris was trying to become invisible, staying silent and still holding a hand over her mouth. Artemis turned her attention to Raphael, searching his face while he was looking at Claude.

"That was our maker, yes." Clearing his throat, Claude found the hole in the wall very fascinating. "She found eternal peace a while ago."

"I killed her." Raphael's words brought heavy silence where it felt like everyone was holding their breath.

"It was deserved," Claude looked at Raphael." I never blamed you for that."

"I couldn't care less who blames me for what, Claude. I never regretted it to this day." Staring intently, Raphael dared Claude to say otherwise. "But that's beside the point. We're talking about the portal and the Fae."

"I told you what I know. Until a week ago, I thought it was all some bullshit story Anissa told to make herself sound more important. You know she loved feeling like she was on top of the world." Claude's eyes kept flicking to Artemis like he was expecting a reaction from her.

She watched him without any expression on her pretty face, making him feel uncomfortable. When Claude realized Raphael was looking at him through narrowed eyes, he straightened his shoulders and stopped looking at her. At least for now, he could pretend that the damn Fae was not holding his attention, even though he felt drawn to her, like a moth to a flame. No matter how hard he tried, his eyes kept going to her. *What was it about Raphael that got her to turn to him and what did he do to change her mind? Instead of hunting us down, she's sitting here chatting like we are old friends,* his mind kept nagging at him.

"Possibly." Reluctantly, Raphael agreed with him.

"Or it's the truth." At her words, they all turned to look at Artemis. Shrugging a shoulder, she dropped her head on the back of the sofa and closed her eyes. "The king's name is Lazarus, and he has been ruling since the death of the queen."

"Your mother?" Raphael gently moved stray hairs away from her face.

"Yes," Artemis whispered, not opening her eyes. Iris gasped and Claude groaned.

"Ah, fuck! I knew those eyes were the ones I've heard about!" Claude fumed. "It's all true, isn't it?"

"Possibly." Artemis repeated Raphael's words from earlier.

"Are you sure?" Iris spoke for the first time, and the look on her face said she was ready to beg for anyone to say this whole thing was a joke. "I mean, how sure are you? Like, sure? Or SURE, sure?"

"You're rambling," Claude pointed out as if she didn't know what she was doing, and she glared at him.

"Thanks, Captain Obvious!" Turning around to squarely face Artemis and Raphael from her seat, Iris ignored Claude. She looked at them with pleading eyes.

Artemis studied her face, tilting her head this way and that. Both vampires stayed silent as the two women remained in a silent conversation for what felt like hours but was probably a minute. The air around them was charged with magic that was prickling their skin like ants crawling on them. Raphael drew lazy circles with his thumb on the back of Artemis's hand as if trying to calm her down. Her fingers tightened in a reassuring gesture on his, making him relax his stiff shoulders.

Raphael was marveling at the change he was experiencing. With each second, he felt more protective and more in tune with her feelings, like some invisible thread was linking them from one to the other. With the good came the bad, too. Like wanting to gouge Claude's eyes out because they kept flicking to Artemis, irritating him to no end.

"A changeling." The corners of Artemis's lips started curling up slowly as Iris's eyes widened comically. "Isn't that a fun development in this mess."

"A what?" Claude's replied with a frown.

"A Fae child switched with a human at birth," Raphael mumbled, looking at Iris with calculating eyes.

"How do you even know this?" Claude looked at him incredulously, but Raphael ignored him.

"Oh, no!" Iris jumped up from her seat, pointing a finger accusingly at him. "You can wipe that stupid look off your face, vampire! Whatever it is that you think I'm going to do, I'll tell you my answer now. It's loud and clear. Read my lips, too! NO!"

"That's why she was able to open that portal," Raphael told Artemis conversationally, and she nodded, still smiling, not looking away from Iris.

"Does anyone even listen to me? Hello!" Iris was looking around frantically, even at Claude, for help, but he only shrugged his shoulders as to tell her she was on her own. "I'm not doing it!" Pursing her lips, she crossed her arms, acting like a petulant child.

"Do you want to know why I lost consciousness earlier?" Artemis asked her softly, and Iris narrowed her eyes but jerked her head in an affirmative nod. "I left my weapon back in my realm. They are using it to pull me back through the portal. With everything that I know now…" her words trailed off.

Iris's eyes narrowed even more as her jaw ticked while she clenched her teeth. Raphael growled low in his throat, too, at that revelation. Artemis stayed focused on Iris without blinking.

"I need to retrieve my weapon or they will pull me through eventually. If that happens, between Lazarus and me …only one will be left standing, and I'm unsure if I'm in a position to face him at the moment. Not like this."

"I'm going with you!" Raphael's words had a finality to

them, making Artemis finally turn her head and look at him.

"You will be killed. You're proof that I'm compromised. It's best to not show our hand from the start. Not until I know the truth." She took special care to sound reasonable and make him understand how stupid that idea was.

"I'm going!" He frowned at her. "I'm not letting you out of my sight...I don't think I can, even if I agreed with you."

"I'll do it!" Groaning and trying to stop the argument that was sure to start, Iris buried her face in her hands. "I'll open the damn portal. You two walk in, grab the weapon and walk out. Thirty seconds! That's all you'll have. After that, they can kill you there for all I care!" Her words, muffled by her fingers, sounded pained.

Chapter Twenty-Five

"Out!"

The words were soft, but there was no mistaking the warning in Raphael's voice. He didn't look away from Artemis as Iris was the first to jump from her seat and bolt through the door like she'd been waiting for the first chance to get out of there. Shaking his head and sighing, Claude followed her, closing the door behind him. Artemis didn't look away. She watched Raphael curiously, wondering what in the world she was doing by allowing this craziness or glitch by the fates to continue. He was her mate. It was unheard of and ridiculous.

Forbidden.

"You think me a monster..."

"I think no such thing." She cut him off. "What is this? All of a sudden you think you know me so well that you know what I think?" Lifting an eyebrow, she waited for his answer.

"I don't regret killing my maker. I cared for her at one point in time, as misguided as that was. But she was a cruel, manipulative abomination and someone needed to do it. I had the honor." Raphael searched her eyes, looking for something she knew he would never find—judgment.

"There is no need for this conversation, Raphael." She watched his eyes burn hot when she said his name, making stupid butterflies flutter in her stomach. He radiated hunger through his entire being, making her heart speed up and her breath shorten. "You forgot that a few days ago, you were hunting a monster." As her head tilted to the side, she smiled at him. "Me!"

"What you did was different. Now that I know your reasons, I can't blame you. The more I learn, the easier it is to justify everything you did. If I am honest, I might say I would've been crueler if our roles had been reversed." One side of his mouth lifted a little as he brought his face closer to her. "I am a monster, too. Compared to me, you are a saint." His breath tickled her lips.

"What is a saint but a sinner who never got caught?" she whispered before his lips crushed hers in a hungry kiss.

Raphael felt possessed.

Hunger like he'd never known before overtook him. Wrapping his arms around her, he dragged her over himself as he devoured her mouth. He had known lust, but this was way beyond any he had felt before. It was an all-consuming need.

His hands roamed her body. Crushing her to himself, he glided them over her sides towards her narrow waist, down to her hips. Sliding his fingers into the waistband of her pants, he didn't stop until he'd pushed them down and his hands had a firm grip on her ass. She moaned throatily in his mouth and a feral sound rumbled in his chest.

Artemis didn't stay docile, either. She gave as much as she got, clawing at his shoulders and ripping his nicely-pressed shirt. A dark, sinister chuckle escaped Raphael as he released her mouth and started trailing kisses from her jaw down her neck. Artemis rocked her hips, pressing harder on his bulging erection while gripping his waist with her thighs. She was breathing harshly and her breath caught in her throat as she felt him drag his fangs down her neck—hard enough to speed up her heart to a whole new level but not hard enough to pierce her skin.

"I will not bite you without permission. You have my word," he panted in her ear before devouring her mouth again.

Artemis lost all ability to think and she gave herself over to her instincts. Exploring his mouth and twining her tongue with his, she tried to take control. A rumble that sounded suspiciously like laughter sounded from Raphael before he flipped them so fast she felt dizzy for a second before she realized that she was pressed, bent over the sofa with Raphael behind her. A ripping sound split the silence and hushed their hard breathing a second before she felt the chilly air on her skin.

It was a peculiar situation for Artemis. She wasn't used to not being the one in control or the stronger one of the two. Yet here she was, bent over, naked, while Raphael was still fully dressed behind her. Preparing herself to argue or push him away, she looked over her shoulder at him, and it felt like everything around her stopped.

Raphael's shirt was open, exposing a glimpse of his chiseled torso as his muscles bunched and jumped with each movement he made. Slowly, as if giving her a show, he took his shirt off and dropped it on the floor. Her mouth watered at the sight. When Artemis tried to move, he pressed one palm on the small of her back, holding her as she was. Her heart sped up and the blood rushing to her ears made so much noise that she felt dizzy.

An arrogant male smirk graced his full lips as he watched her, holding her still one-handed. Painfully slowly, his other hand went to the belt of his pants. Artemis zeroed in on that like it was the most fascinating thing in the world. Her channel clutched emptiness as heat pooled low in her belly. She watched the belt slide slowly loop after loop until it was in Raphael's hand. Before realizing what he was up to, Artemis found that belt looped around both her wrists as he wrapped the other end around his wrist.

"No running away for you now." He whispered harshly in her ear just as she heard the sound of the zipper being lowered. Her insides clenched and she felt herself trembling in anticipation.

Raphael was holding on to a thin thread. His entire body was coiled like a spring, waiting to snap at any moment. He wanted to give her time to be ready for him. He should've known better. She was a predator just like him. As soon as the zipper was lowered and he pushed his pants halfway down his hips, she jerked her body back, pushing her ass on his erection, and he almost physically felt his control snap. He was so hard that it bordered on painful as his cock jerked at the skin contact and the heat that radiated from between her thighs.

With one hand pressed next to her shoulder on the sofa and holding the belt, he wrapped his other arm around her waist, lifting her slightly before embedding himself to the hilt. Both of them moaned deep and long. She was tight like a glove around him, making him wish to stay like that forever. She threw her head back, closing her eyes, and her lush lips were parted as he watched her over her shoulder. Sliding his hand up her belly, Raphael filled it with her breast, his fingers pinching and teasing her nipple. Artemis became restless and started wiggling her hips a second before he pulled almost all the way out and then slammed back in one jerk of his hips.

Artemis felt full to the brim. It should be even painful, but it felt too good for her to be able to feel anything but pleasure. Raphael was a large male, and she should've known that large worked in all aspects for the vampire. Her legs were shaking and his arms caging her were the only thing holding her up. The sounds of skin slapping skin were echoing around the room, and the scent that was making her dizzy was so potent it made her want to claw out of her skin. Now she knew it was Raphael's scent that she reacted to, not a weapon.

Lifting her lower body almost off the sofa, Raphael changed the angle, getting even deeper inside her with his thrusts, and the sounds she was making were driving him insane. His fangs throbbed in his mouth but he ignored them. Liquid was gathering in her and was running down his thighs as he kept a relentless tempo. She was getting close to her orgasm as her channel started quivering and tightening around him and he sped up his thrusts. Determined to push her over the edge and still keep his word, he kept his face away from her. Piercing the inside of his mouth, he groaned at the taste of his own blood as he was inside Artemis. His eyes burned bright amber, casting orange shadows on her back. He thought he was good, under control. Then she tilted her head, baring her throat to him. He froze.

Artemis didn't know what possessed her. Whatever it was, she was all instinct, and it felt right. She bared her throat and expected him to attack like a savage. But he froze, and she turned her head to look at him over her shoulder. He looked fierce and terrifying. His body was glistening with sweat, his hair was falling over his forehead and there was a look of determination on his face that took her breath away. He searched her face. She watched him for a moment longer before turning her head and baring her throat again.

"Are you sure?" His voice was deeper than she had ever heard it and his words were slurred by the fangs.

Without answering, she pushed her hips back, causing friction that made them both moan. One second. That was all the time he gave her. Pistoning his hips, he brought her to the edge many times until she was ready to beg. She felt his breath on her shoulder before the butterfly kiss made her stop breathing. She was so close. The rubber band was pulled beyond its limits in her belly, ready to snap. Then, as she felt his fangs pierce her skin, the most intense pleasure made her burst into million pieces. Lights flashed behind her closed eyelids and she thought she heard herself scream Raphael's name, but she couldn't be sure. What she was sure about was Raphael's roar of her name as she summoned enough strength to look over her shoulder and see him at the peak of his passion. His eyes were closed and his head was thrown back, muscles bunched up as if ready for an attack. His lips were parted with his fangs gleaming as her blood ran in rivulets down his chin and neck. He finally looked down at her, and his eyes lost the hunger as they softened. Artemis closed her eyes and drifted to sleep with a slight smile on her face.

Chapter Twenty-Six

"Where is the male?" Claude glared at Iris, getting angrier by the second because she refused to answer any of his questions.

"He is not here, as I've told you ten times by now!" she looked at everything else but him.

"You're hiding him from me because you're one of them. Aren't you, witch?"

"No! And I said to leave me alone!" Iris snapped at Claude. "Everyone has a right to say whatever they want. It doesn't mean it's true."

Pacing across the large room, she wondered how smart it was to have brought the deranged vampire to a place that had been soundproofed, cut off from everything around it. She just needed some time away from everyone, time to think about all the implications that came with Artemis's revelation.

Claude, on the other hand, was happy that the witch had finally brought him to her ritual room, since here he didn't have to listen to the sounds of sex that almost drove him insane. It took him a while to convince her, but when she started feeling uncomfortable herself and started shifting in the seat, she relented. In this room, he could finally think about everything that had been said earlier. He told them the gist of it, but not everything. He wasn't even sure about all the details, but he knew one thing for sure. Anissa couldn't shut up about the effect Fae blood had on vampires. That's why she was so obsessed with opening that portal. Until vampires started dropping like flies, Claude thought all that was just a bullshit story told by a psychotic bitch. His ambitions to stay on top of the game proved beneficial once again. Only an idiot will pass on any information. No matter how insignificant it seemed at the time, it can come in handy. Like it did right now.

"The bug didn't sound confused..." Looking at Iris contemplatively, he mused as his handsome face morphed into a mask of deadly beauty. "As a matter a fact, she sounded very certain."

"She's guessing. It's all stories told to little children. Changeling, my ass. And you do know I'll tell Raphael that you keep calling Artemis a bug, right? It'll be fun to watch him dangle you around like a dog with a bone." Iris gloated even as her brain was screaming at her to shut up and leave him alone.

"Not if I drain you right here, you won't." A cruel smile split Claude's lips as she took a step back. "I've heard that blood of the Fae is an aphrodisiac for us. If what she said is true..." His words trailed off as he took one step towards her.

"You wouldn't dare!" Iris hated the fact that her fear was evident in her voice as she took another step back. "They need me to open the portal. Raphael will rip you limb from limb and you know it!"

"Like I give a fuck! Who will stop me now, witch? It's just you and me here." Lifting an eyebrow Claude took another determined step towards her.

Iris tried to run. With her heart in her throat, she bolted towards the door, but Claude was a vampire. He moved as fast as the wind and as silent as death. She hadn't taken two steps before he slammed into her back and together they hit the closed door at such a speed that Iris almost lost consciousness as all the air from her lungs was pushed out.

Grabbing a handful of her long hair, Claude wrapped it around his hand, jerking her head back as he rasped his fangs over her neck. The urge to hunt made him as hard as a rock and he nestled his cock in her round ass, pressing her more firmly to the door. Feeling how she trembled in his hands made him want to start gorging on her blood until there wasn't even a drop left. He knew that everything that happened tonight had gotten to him and this wasn't something he normally did. There were enough willing humans around that he didn't need to attack anyone for it. But the fear he felt because of Raphael had made him angry. The attraction he felt towards Artemis, while she ignored him, made him livid, and the witch taunting him only made it worse. He needed to feel like his usual self, respected and feared as he should be. Draining the witch would make him feel better, if nothing else. Somewhere in the back of his mind was this little voice telling him that hurting her was an idiotic idea that could get him killed, but he was beyond rational thought.

"Raphael!" The piercing scream that ripped from her throat made Claude loosen his grip as he stumbled back, covering the closest ear with his hand. "Help!" Iris kept screaming.

Venus Trap

"Shut up!" Claude snapped at Iris, backhanding her and sending her sprawling on the floor.

Iris tried to lift herself off the ground, but her chest was hurting like she had a broken rib and her face was throbbing as she tasted blood in her mouth. Twice she tried to push herself up and twice she failed, dropping down to press her cheek on the cold floor. Tears streamed down her face as her vision blurred. *This can't be the end. I can't die now.* Her mind sounded as desperate as she felt. Through the curtain of her hair that covered her face, she watched Claude's shoes as he started coming closer. The click, click, of the shoes on the floor was like nails in her brain as fear clogged her throat and she found herself unable to breathe. Her fear made her release control of whatever beast had been sleeping inside her since the day she was born. She could almost physically feel it stretching and purring in her head, as if satisfied with her decision to let it loose. All the gods and the universe help them now that has been unleashed.

"Ancestors, don't fail me now," She murmured under her breath, gasping for air as energy started swirling in her chest like a tornado. "Hear my desperate plea, heed my call. When witch's blood is spilled, payment is taken from all."

Stopping where Iris was curled up on the floor, Claude crouched next to her. "What did you say, witch?" Moving her hair out of her face with his fingers, his fangs throbbed at the smell of her blood.

He had only enough time to lock eyes with her. Green eyes were burning with rage and so much power that it almost made Claude fall back on his ass. A blast of magic slammed into him, sending him careening back to the other side of the room. His body wrapped around one of the silver statues, almost bending awkwardly in half before he dropped, unmoving, to the floor. Iris lifted her head slightly, just enough to make sure that he wasn't moving. Before losing consciousness herself, the last thing she remembered was the door banging open and rushed footsteps coming her way. It might have been a foe, but she couldn't stay awake even if it meant that she would die this night.

Chapter Twenty-Seven

The magic being unleashed made Raphael hiss in pain as he bolted upright. He was holding Artemis wrapped around his body, enjoying the feel of her skin on his, but this ruined his moment of peace. His reaction made her sit upright as well, looking around, alert, as if she hadn't been in a deep sleep a second ago.

"What in the world was that?" Her eyes connected with Raphael's.

"Iris!" Raphael was gone the next second, making Artemis's hair fly around her face as the door slammed against the opposite wall before swinging a few times.

Without waiting, Artemis followed him. After their passionate moments, she felt much better instead of exhausted. She found it strange that her body was guiding her towards him, out of her control—as if she knew where he was even when she couldn't see him. Her skin was itching and felt tight with the urge to shift, but she pushed it down. As her feet brought her to the door of the ritual room, she slowed down.

Raphael was standing butt naked in front of a heap on the floor, glaring towards one of the silver statues. Her eyes followed his muscular frame as his arms bulged while he clenched his fists, baring his fangs at the statue and confusing her. His firm ass was trying to get her attention as heat pooled in her belly at the magnificent creature in front of her, but she knew that she had to focus. The vampire would be the death of her if he kept on making her check him out instead of paying attention to the danger that was making him look almost feral.

The magic was still active as if an intelligent entity was present with them in the room, but Artemis didn't feel threatened—unlike Raphael, who kept hissing while his eyes burned amber. Crossing over the threshold, she strolled towards Raphael, not making a sound. All her senses were on alert, but still, no danger could be detected.

"Raphael?" she spoke softly, as she placed her hand on his arm, wrapping her fingers around the rock-hard muscle that was so tense it felt like she was touching marble. "I don't sense any danger here. What is it that I can't see?" Her eyes scanned the room.

Raphael didn't answer her, but he pushed Artemis behind his back as if protecting her from the invisible foe, still glaring at the statue. Confused, she moved slightly to look around him in the hope she would see whatever it is he was looking at. That was when another lump on the floor, this one at the foot of the statue, stirred slightly, making her tense up.

Reaching behind him, Raphael wrapped his arm around Artemis, pressing her against his back. That was when his brain took over from his instincts. Then he felt her press her skin on his back. The crazy Fae was as naked as he was, and that sobered him up faster than a bucket of water.

He started looking around for something to cover her up when she glided her hands over his back and it felt like his entire being was on fire. His cock got hard and lust started clouding his mind.

"Keep touching me like that and I'll fuck you first, *then* I'll see what happened here to Iris and Claude." His voice was deep and she felt its vibrations through his back, making her squeeze her thighs together. "I can smell your need. It's not helping at the moment."

Turning around, Raphael had every intention on following on his promise, but he found no one there. Artemis, hearing him mention Iris and Claude, was on her knees, turning Iris onto her back and checking for injuries. When he saw Iris's face, he went closer to see for himself.

"Who attacked her here?" Artemis looked over at Raphael with a frown on her face. "She's alive, but I thought she was safe here...with him," she mumbled, jerking her head towards the other lump that she assumed was Claude.

A groan was heard from Claude a second before he started moving sluggishly, slowly sitting up. Artemis ignored him as she scanned Iris with her hands and eyes. Her breathing was labored and a bruise was forming on one side of her face where her lip was split.

"Who did this to you?" Artemis whispered as anger bubbled up in her chest. "Who hurt you while I was here to protect you?"

"I know who did it." Raphael's angry growl made Artemis look at him sharply as he gently moved the hair away from the witch's face. In contradiction to his angry words, his thumb ran gently over an imprint on her swollen cheek.

Artemis frowned, looking closer at it, when the air

stirred and she heard a crash on the other side of the room. Rolling her eyes, she sat back on her haunches and turned around to see Raphael holding Claude by the neck. This was rapidly becoming a typical interaction between the two vampires. The strange thing was that Claude was not trying to defend himself. He was looking at Raphael, wide-eyed, as if seeing him for the first time. Raphael must've noticed it too, because his hand came down slowly before he turned to look at her with confusion on his face.

"Who are you?" Claude's whispered words made both Raphael and Artemis exchange a puzzled look. "Where am I?" He looked around the room like he was seeing it for the first time.

This was bad. Very bad!

"Don't play stupid with me, Claude." Raphael turned to look at Claude while speaking through clenched teeth. "I will rip your head off your shoulders if you don't start talking. And the reason the witch is unconscious with an imprint of your ring on her swollen face had better be the best reason you've had in your entire life!"

Claude's eyes widened even more, if that was possible, as he swallowed thickly and looked at Artemis for the first time. She was sitting unnaturally still, her eyes glowing like violet flames on her beautiful face. Claude swayed towards her before Raphael grabbed him by the neck again. Veins bulged on Claude's neck.

"He's telling the truth." Artemis's softly spoken words stopped Raphael from finally killing Claude. "I don't know what happened, but in defending herself, I think Iris used ancient magic." Tilting her head, she studied Claude. "She didn't kill him, which tells me she had a reason to keep him alive. I'd say we wait until she wakes up." Locking eyes with Raphael, a predatory smile lifted her lips. "If she doesn't care if he lives or dies, you can kill him then." Her smile grew as Claude started to tremble visibly.

Looking back at Claude, Raphael had a terrible feeling about this whole shitstorm "You better start praying that she has something to say on your behalf," he told the bewildered vampire. "Although after seeing her, I doubt you should hold out much hope."

Chapter Twenty-Eight

"It feels strange," Artemis told Raphael as she looked down at what she was wearing.

"You look stunning," he reassured her.

Raphael had brought the dress from the store after they made Iris as comfortable as she could be and he was adamant that she put it on. Apparently in this realm, they looked down on the naked form. It clung to her curves like a second skin, flaring at her hips and covering only half her thighs. She watched him look at her with hunger in his eyes, so she didn't complain about it. Artemis was used to her pants that felt like a second skin, because she could move in them when fighting. A frown formed on her face as she realized her entire life had been spent fighting and nothing more. Now, with all the revelations, her whole existence had been turned upside down, and she was sure that denial was firm in her mind. Otherwise, she might go insane. There was no other explanation for the way she was so calm and going along with everything around her.

"Did you hear me, beautiful?" Cupping her face in his

palm, Raphael smoothed her frown with his fingers. He must've been talking while she was stuck in her mind. "What's wrong?" Her stomach tightened at the worry in his eyes as he searched her face.

"You forget who you're worried about, Raphael." She looked at him soberly. "I'm not a fragile human that you need to fret about."

"I can't help but be worried." He kissed her forehead, making her eyes close. "I can't have anything happen to you." Moving back a little, he watched her until her eyes opened. "I wouldn't survive that."

"I'm not hurt, Iris is, and we need her to open the portal. You should worry about her."

At her words, Raphael released her face and turned towards the witch, who was sleeping on the sofa. Kneeling down next to her head, he pulled the sleeve of his shirt up, exposing his wrist. As his fangs elongated and he opened his mouth ready to bite, a fit of inexplicable jealousy overwhelmed Artemis.

"No!" Her words were like a whip, and Raphael froze an inch from his wrist before slowly turning his head to look at her. "No," Artemis repeated softly, a confused look on her face.

"I was only going to give her a drop so she could heal faster." He frowned at his own words before focusing on Artemis again. "Although, I must say, I feel unlike myself after tasting your blood."

"Unlike yourself in what way?" She tilted her head looking him over. "My whole life I've been told that vampires crave our blood like a drug. Is that what you're feeling? Just how the humans crave our jewels for power. I didn't think of that when I let you bite me."

In an instant, she was wrapped in Raphael's arms as he

looked down at her. "I crave you, Artemis. Not your blood *or* your jewels. You!" Crushing her to his chest, he took her breath away with a passionate kiss. "I crave you more with each passing second," he told her as they came up for breath. He smiled at her unfocused gaze.

"I think I'm going to be sick." Iris groaned from behind them. "Either from the pain or the cheesy vampire, one or the other." she mumbled under her breath.

"I don't understand how you can be sick of Raphael." Artemis frowned at Iris. "I didn't let him give you his blood."

Making a gagging sound, wincing, Iris lifted herself to a sitting position. "Thank the gods you didn't. Now I really think I'm going to be sick."

"What happened in that room, witch?" Snatching a glass of water from the table, Raphael handed it to Iris. "And what's wrong with Claude?"

At his words, Iris dropped the glass that she was bringing to her lips. Water splashed all over her and the sofa, but her body turned cold and shivers crawled up her spine, making her numb with fear. Her face drained of all color and Artemis moved fast to grab her arm and hold her up as her body started falling to one side. Raphael and Artemis looked at each other before focusing again on Iris.

"What happened, Iris?" Artemis turned Iris's head so that their eyes were locked. "No one can hurt you, I promise you that. Tell me what happened."

"He kept pushing me to confirm your words." In a monotone voice, Iris spoke through numb lips. "He said he would drain me. I tried to run…he's fast, I couldn't get away…" Her words trailed off as her body started shaking and her breaths were coming short and fast. "I don't know what happened after that. I was only trying to protect myself." Her eyes looked frantically from Artemis to Raphael and back.

"Breathe, witch. No one is going to hurt you. That Claude is not here." Raphael reassured her, but uneasiness twisted his gut. "He doesn't even remember who I am, if it's any consolation."

"What?" Iris stopped gasping for air as she stared at Raphael, openmouthed. Wincing, she closed her mouth as she pressed the back of her hand against her split lip. "The asshole did a number on me," she snarled, glaring and clenching her fists in her lap.

"Since you're alive, Claude is the least of my concerns at the moment. I don't think we can delay opening the portal until you have time to properly heal." Putting his hands in his pockets, he leaned his behind against the table as he watched Iris intently. She squirmed where she sat.

"When I got here, I was in worse shape than you and I didn't think to ask." Artemis confused them with her comment as she kept her eyes on Iris. "Where is Fern?"

"Who?" Raphael's mind took a screeching halt at the worried expression on Artemis's face.

"The male that came through the portal with me." She didn't look away from Iris "Where is he? Is he alive?"

A growl rumbled inside Raphael's chest as his eyes started glowing amber, making Iris forget all about the pain she was feeling. Waving her arms to get his attention from its focus solely on Artemis, she prayed that Raphael wouldn't go searching for the Fae. Artemis, oblivious of the jealous vampire, tilted her head, watching Iris like she was the strangest creature in the universe.

"You're her mate, remember!" Iris forced her voice as loud as she could. "Yo! Raphael! She said you're her mate."

Looking over her shoulder, Artemis finally saw the angry

vampire staring daggers at her. For some reason, knowing that he was jealous of Fern made her smile at him. His glare deepened as her smile grew. Ignoring Iris as she muttered something about supernatural creatures being the death of her, Artemis stood up and walked up to him. Placing both palms on his chest, she looked at him through her lashes.

"You would fight for me, vampire? To keep me at your side?" she purred at him, and his arms wrapped around her so tightly she couldn't take a full breath.

"If he's still alive and you want to keep him that way, I suggest you convince me real fast that he means nothing to you." Through clenched teeth, Raphael's deep voice vibrated from his chest to hers.

"Is he alive, Iris?" she asked, not looking away from Raphael.

"Yes?" the word coming out of Iris was more a question than an answer as she looked at the vampire apprehensively.

"Good!" Artemis purred next to Raphael's ear. "You can show me how hard you will fight for your mate." Biting gently on his ear, she soothed it with the tip of her tongue.

"All of you are insane!" Iris said incredulously. "You made her as insane as you are!" she said, pointing an accusing finger at Raphael and glaring at him.

One side of Raphael's lips twitched as he fought a smile. "It's her instincts telling her she needs me to prove I'm a worthy mate." He lost the battle and his smile grew, but it was anything but a nice smile. Iris's own instincts of fight or flight were hitting her full force. "I will prove my worth the first chance I get."

Chapter Twenty-Nine

Artemis was starting to get anxious to get out of the witch's place. It felt like she'd been sitting here for an eternity. Raphael had left a while ago to take Claude to his mansion and hide him there from the rest of their kind. She knew how many of them lived in that monstrosity of a house, and she wondered how he was planning to accomplish that. A slight smile ghosted her lips. Raphael would most definitely find a way. The vampire was more determined than anyone she'd ever met.

Snatching a piece of apple from the bowl that Iris left before disappearing to check on things, Artemis's mind went back to what Claude had told them earlier that evening. If she believed his words, that meant that Lazarus, her father, killed her mother while he fed Artemis stories that the humans and vampires were to blame. Their entire realm knew that to be a fact. All Fae despised humans for banishing them and closing the portal. Armies trained for centuries, preparing for the day the veil would lift.

Her eyes were unfocused as she nibbled on the apple.

The sweetness of the crisp fruit was lost to her as her stomach started churning. It would not be a fight or a war. For centuries, the Fae had stewed in anger and resentment. No, it would not be a war, it would be a slaughter, and here she was contemplating on how to stop it. Artemis shook her head as a snort escaped her lips.

"How life can change in a blink of an eye," she murmured under her breath.

In one day, Artemis had changed her focus from trying to find a way to escape to trying to find a way to keep everyone here alive. At first she'd thought finding her mate was what brought the change, but if she were honest with herself, she had to admit that she'd started to care. Iris and Raphael were to blame. Even when they knew that their lives were in danger, both of them had showed her kindness, something that no one had previously demonstrated to Artemis. There were some that had been nice and helpful through the years, but always while they were expecting something in return—mostly to get on the right side of Lazarus. The witch and the vampire took care of her even when they knew that the moment she opened her eyes, she could kill them, and probably would. Her mind was a mess, but Artemis knew that she would do everything in her power to keep them safe.

"That's a lot of heavy thinking." Iris smiled at her as Artemis turned to look her way "I can hear those gears turning from across the hall."

"Sometimes you say things that make no sense to me." Rubbing her hands over her face, Artemis leaned back in her chair. "Do you do that to confuse me?"

Snorting and pulling the chair across from her, Iris grabbed a piece of apple as well. "Most of the time I confuse myself. Don't feel special." She watched Artemis for a moment, chewing thoughtfully. "What are you thinking? And before you tell me 'nothing,' think again. I can feel the tension as a physical presence in this room." Reaching a hand, she squeezed gently on Artemis's hand. "Do you want to talk about it?"

"I want to say so much... I also want to say nothing." With a sigh, Artemis searched Iris's face. "I don't know exactly when I started caring, but I want to prevent what's coming. It seems like I've been lied to my whole life, and I need to get to the bottom of it. How I can do that and make sure you're safe? I don't know. I don't know if I can stop what's coming."

"What do you mean, what's coming?" Widening her eyes, Iris moved forward until she almost sat at the edge of her chair.

"Iris, the Fae have been preparing themselves to cross over for a very long time. We were told the humans chose to side with the vampires, so they killed our queen and closed the portal, banishing us forever. For centuries we've been training and trying to lift the veil so we can seek revenge." Artemis told her soberly.

"Oh, dear gods..." Open-mouthed, Iris gaped at Artemis while her heart forgot how to beat.

"I need your help." Waiting until Iris nodded while still looking wide-eyed, Artemis looked intently into the other woman's eyes. "I need you to distract Raphael so that I can go through the portal alone."

"Are you crazy?" Iris jumped off the chair. "You want him to kill me? Hell, no!"

"If he comes with me to my realm, he will die!" Artemis snapped at her. "He is my mate, and I have to do what I must to protect him. You will do as I say or all of you will die! Don't you understand, witch?"

"How can I possibly keep a vampire distracted?" Sitting back down, Iris pinched the bridge of her nose, hoping to stop the headache she felt coming on. "How the hell I always manage to get myself into shit like this is beyond me."

"I just need to go back to get my weapon and see if I can find information that can help us. I'm in half mind to pretend that I was held captive and I escaped in hopes that Lazarus will tell me something. Is Fern awake? Can we talk to him?"

"No." Iris shook her head sadly "He is alive, but he is not waking up. I tried everything. At least, he is alive."

"He broke a sworn oath to Lazarus. Only my father, or my father's death, can free him from it."

"Holy shit!" Iris gasped. "We were talking about the queen being killed by her consort and you being her daughter, but it never dawned on me that he's actually your father. Dude, that's really messed up!"

"Huh?" Tilting her head, Artemis frowned slightly at those words.

"Never mind, I talk like a blathering idiot when I get shocked by something." Iris waved away the confusion. "At least that's good news. We know he won't kill you if you go back." She looked at Artemis for a second before frowning. "What?"

"Lazarus cares about Lazarus, nothing else," Artemis told her. "If he suspects me of anything, it's a serious possibility there will be a battle, and only one of us will survive it."

"That's one more reason you shouldn't go alone. I've kind of started liking you, to tell you the truth. Besides, you make the vampire less annoying." Iris chuckled awkwardly. "I would hate to have anything happen to you."

"What could happen to someone like me when you know what I am?" Artemis smiled slightly.

"What do you mean, what you are?" Iris looked at her, confused. It wasn't Artemis that answered.

"A weapon." Raphael joined their conversation while leaning his shoulder on the doorway.

A high-pitched scream ripped from Iris's throat. "Oh, my God, you scared the shit out of me!" She glared at him. Raphael ignored her.

"Isn't that so, Artemis?" His green eyes were locked on Artemis as she turned to look at him.

"It is." Her eyes flashed in a challenge.

"How long have you been standing there?" Iris asked him, accusation evident in her voice.

"Long enough to tell you that you don't need to worry about distracting me." He narrowed his eyes at Iris for a second before looking back at Artemis. "And you are not going anywhere alone!"

With a groan, Iris folded her arms on the table, and leaning down, thumped her forehead on it.

Chapter Thirty

Raphael was fuming inside while trying his best to keep his calm façade. He knew before leaving to hide Claude that Artemis was plotting something. He could see it in her mesmerizing eyes and in the way she was distracted and very still. He found it astounding that in such a short time he'd learned to pick up little things like that. Regardless of whether it was the mate bond making it possible or not, he was happy to take whatever he could if that meant he would keep her at his side. With each passing moment the need became stronger, and it was almost turning into an obsession.

It was fear, he had to admit to himself, which was ludicrous. He hadn't felt fear for so long until he saw the Fae for the first time that it took him a while to recognize it. What a peculiar feeling that was, fear. Pushing himself off the doorframe and shaking his head slightly, Raphael walked into the room and headed straight to where Artemis was sitting, watching him warily. It felt like the two women were holding their breath to see what he would do next.

Raphael stepped so close to Artemis she had to spread her legs as he stepped between them and cupped her face, lifting it up so he could look at her eyes. He noticed the way her face tilted into his touch on instinct, and his lips quirked at the corners while her eyes flashed at him in defiance. It was not going to be an easy argument to win. Oh, no! He was sure of that, but he had yet to meet anyone who could outwit him when he had his mind set on something. In this case, it wasn't just his mind but his heart and everything else that was set on Artemis.

"Where you go, I go." Raphael spoke softly, searching her eyes. "With everything that we know now, you cannot possibly expect me to sit back and wait while you place your life in danger."

"It will not be I who is in danger, Raphael!" She frowned as if she couldn't believe that he couldn't see that.

"Yes, it will! And you keep forgetting I'm not human." His eyes hardened, making hers narrow at him. "I will not sit back and wait to see if you live or die!"

"It's the mate bond…"

"It has nothing to do with the mate bond!" He cut her off, stepping away from her angrily. "I've sat back and left the world to evolve around me for too long! Look where it got us all! People I've known my entire existence are dead! Claude is in some deep shit I knew nothing about, and it can kill us all!" Clenching his fists, he seemed almost to grow in size with the anger radiating from him. "I will not sit back on this! If it gets me killed, so be it!"

"I think you two need to sort this out, so I'll go check on Fern…or something." Iris lifted herself from the chair, clapping her hands together like some preschool teacher. She smiled tightly at them as she hurried out of the room.

"Wait, Iris! Can I see him?" Artemis jumped up from

the chair and a growl came from Raphael's chest while his eyes flashed amber. The hairs on the back of Iris's neck stood on end as she froze at the door. Artemis, on the other hand, just smiled wickedly at Raphael.

Shaking her head and muttering under her breath, Iris left the room, closing the door behind her with a thump. Still smiling at Raphael, Artemis leaned on the table and crossed her arms. He stood with his clenched fists and a scowl on his handsome face, making her shift uncomfortably. He was breathtaking in his jealousy, fierce and possessive.

"Don't test me, woman!" He practically growled the words as her smile grew. "Now is not the time. I keep saying you mistake me for a human or the fairy boys you are used to."

"You're different." Cocking her head, she looked him over from head to toe as if trying to find a physical difference. "I feel your power much more strongly all around me. And you are not as calm as you were when I saw you a few days ago. It still doesn't mean you can survive everything that comes your way."

"Don't change the subject!"

"I'm not changing anything," Lifting her hand to stop his argument, her eyes narrowed, scrutinizing him. "I'm still talking about how smart, or how stupid, it is to go with me."

"There's nothing to talk about." Walking up to her, he pressed her body between the table and his muscled chest, making her breath quicken. "Where you go, I go! End of story!"

To stop any further arguments, Raphael took her mouth in a searing kiss. One of his arms wrapped like a boa around her waist, lifting her up so she was seated on the table, while his other hand tangled in her hair, tilting it the way he wanted. Everything she tried to say disappeared when his tongue tangled with hers, and she wrapped her legs around his hips, pulling him closer to her. The dress she was wearing bunched up at her hips as she grabbed the back of his head with one hand and clawed at his back with the other. Every time they touched it felt like it wasn't enough.

Releasing her hair, Raphael trailed kisses down from her neck to her shoulder while his hands gripped the neckline and dragged the dress down, exposing her to his hungry mouth and roaming hands. He nipped and licked her skin, driving her crazy as she arched her body, giving him more access and rocking her aching core on his hardness pressed there. Raphael rolled his hips, grinding harder and groaning at her moans. Sucking a nipple in his mouth, he looked up at her tilted face and parted lips. She was too tame at the moment, and he wanted her to feel as out of control as he felt.

Panting and feeling like she wants to claw out of her skin, Artemis looked down and locked eyes with Raphael. Her breath caught in her throat at the raw need and hunger she saw there. He held her captive, and she couldn't look away as he released her nipple and pushed her down on the table while he trailed kisses between her breasts and down her belly. Artemis couldn't breathe as his hands slid under her, lifting her up towards his wicked mouth. She saw it then. In his eyes it was as plain as a day, the determination to get things done his way, no matter what. She was way too far gone to deny him anything and he knew it as well. His smile grew, making her insides clench the emptiness she wanted him to fill a moment before his mouth descended on her aching core.

Raphael didn't move slowly, teasingly or gently. As soon

as he saw the realization dawn in her eyes about his tactics, he attacked her sopping core with vigor, like he was a starving man and she was a feast. He licked, sucked and nibbled between her thighs until the moans started getting louder. It was like music to his ears as he feasted and her hips undulated on his face. When she started getting impatient and her legs squeezed around his head as her hand gripped and pulled on his hair, Raphael pushed two thick digits into her channel, turning her loud moans into screams. She was close, but so was he.

Lifting himself up and not letting her look away from him, he licked his lips as he pulled on his belt and zipper, yanking down his pants and letting his cock spring free from the confinement as her eyes snapped in that direction. His cock jutted out as Artemis licked her dry lips, unable to look away from it. It almost looked angry it was so red, leaking precum and pointing at her accusingly for its state. Wrapping his hand at the base of it, Raphael positioned himself at her entrance, pushing only the tip inside her before stopping.

"What are you doing? Don't stop!" Moaning desperately, she looked at his face, her eyes unfocused, pleading and frantic.

"Where you go, I go!" Raphael was holding onto his control by a thread and his legs were trembling, but he would be damned if he didn't take advantage of this situation to make sure he stayed by her side.

"Fuck me, Raphael! Stop talking!" she moaned and pleaded while her hips kept moving and her hot channel clenched around the head of his cock as if trying to suck him in.

"Promise me, Artemis! I'll give you what you want if you just promise me that!" he growled, wondering if she would be cunning enough to keep him waiting longer. He would fail then, there was no doubt.

Artemis locked eyes with him and he knew at that moment that nothing would ever be the same again for either of them. There was anger in her eyes, but also gratitude, hope, determination and dare he say, something like love. Her beautiful eyes softened and a sad smile ghosted her lips.

"I promise. Where I go, you go." Her husky words were like a healing balm to the fear that had been gnawing at him.

As soon as Artemis made her promise, Raphael slammed inside her with one jerk of his hips, making her scream and bow her body, almost lifting herself off the table. It was so erotic and satisfying that he released the control he'd been holding since he touched her. Grabbing her hips in a bruising grip with both hands, Raphael pistoned so fast that his body started blurring at the edges.

There was something different this time when Raphael was inside her. Artemis was too lost in her passion to be able to figure out what that was, but there was no mistaking the intensity of it or the power swirling around them both. He was a large man, but it felt like he was getting thicker and longer inside her with each thrust of his hips. It was bordering on pleasure-pain and it was making her delirious.

Raphael could feel their mate bond getting settled at last. It was the reason their lovemaking was so intense to a point he thought that after he filled her up, he would disincarnate. She clung to him with her legs around his waist, and he couldn't stop or slow down to save his life. His sack tightened as he felt her walls fluttering around his cock. Bending down over her, he kissed her once where her neck meets her shoulder before sinking his fangs as deep as his cock was in her. The moment her blood touched his tongue, they both exploded. She screamed his name for a long time before he lifted his head and roared hers.

It felt like it lasted forever, their souls' twining and linking as their physical bodies were connected. When they both came down from the pleasure high, Raphael lifted his head to look at her face. He would remember the smile on her face for as long as he lived. That was one second before his eyes widened at the loud cracking sound and they both dropped to the floor with the broken table. Artemis was sound asleep, not noticing anything. Raphael rolled onto his back, pulling her over his chest as he chuckled weakly.

Chapter Thirty-One

The curtains were pulled tightly together and thick blankets had been placed over them to keep the sunlight out of the room. Artemis was pacing like a caged animal while Raphael slept, stretched out on the sofa that looked like a toy compared to his massive body. Her eyes kept going to him no matter how hard she tried to stop herself. She would have to wait until nightfall for him to wake up so that they could go to her realm. Iris was preparing everything to open the portal in her ritual room.

They could've used the portal in the forest, but Raphael said it was better not to. Apparently the vampires thought that Claude was with Artemis, trying to find out everything she knew so he could stop the Fae. With a snort, she kept on pacing. She wasn't sure what the truth was anymore, but regardless, Artemis still thought it might've been a good idea to kill those poor creatures that lived in Claude's mansion. That house stank of greed and sin. Her eyes strayed to Raphael again.

In sleep, his face was relaxed and looked so innocent that it was almost boyish. The chestnut hair was mussed, falling over his forehead as his lips were parted slightly, the lower one fuller than the upper. Her mind went back to what that mouth could do to her and she stopped pacing to press her thighs together as her core started throbbing instantly. The vampire would be the death of her. She wouldn't die in a fight or seeking revenge, as she'd always thought; she would die from need. Artemis had been told that vampires got addicted to Fae blood. No one ever mentioned Fae getting addicted to vampires. And she was addicted! To his touch, his eyes, to his voice. A heavy sigh escaped her parted lips and she shook her head at the craziness of the situation.

Irritated and feeling helpless to come up with a good solution, she yanked on her hair, smoothing it out and twisting it into a braid. Instead of thinking how to take them in and out of her realm alive, her mind kept replaying images of Raphael's naked body glistening in the lights as his muscles bunched up while he thrust in her. Even while he slept, she couldn't control herself and wanted to start removing his clothes and molest him.

"I can feel your need, beautiful," Raphael rasped, his voice thick from sleep. "Come here." He reached his hand towards her, opening one eye to look at her as a slight smile lifted his lips.

"I thought you didn't wake up during the day," she mumbled as her feet took her towards him of their own accord.

"I don't." Taking hold of her hand, he pulled her down and wrapped his body around her. "But as I said, I felt your need. It triggers my own." He tilted his hips and she felt him hard against her thigh.

"Sorry, I don't know what's wrong with me. It's the mating, I think. It's driving me insane at times when I need to stay focused for all our sakes." Artemis closed her eyes as if pained by that knowledge.

"I'm not complaining." Raphael nuzzled her neck before placing butterfly kisses there, making her groan. He chuckled.

"Be serious for a second!" She pushed with her shoulder to dislodge him.

Lifting his head, Raphael looked at her and there was no trace of a smile anywhere. "I'm very serious, I assure you. I find nothing funny when your safety is in question."

"I feel the same when it comes to your safety." He sighed when she cupped his face and he nuzzled her palm. "I need to know that if anything goes wrong, you will get out of there." He looked at her sharply and opened his mouth to say something, but she spoke over him. "Iris will hold the portal open for as long as she can unless someone tries to walk through it. I need to know you will leave if we find ourselves in a bad situation."

"I'm not leaving you behind!" Frowning at her, he pushed himself up and stood. "Are you insane? You think I can just turn my back and leave you to die?"

"Raphael, I don't know what makes you triggered about leaving me behind or whatever it is that you're feeling. I'm not whoever it was that made you feel that guilt that you're trying to redeem through me." Standing up as well, Artemis walked up to him and grabbed his face in both hands. "I will not die! He will not kill me even if I wish that he would. I'm his weapon and he will not lose that! But you? He'll kill you, and if he notices that I care for you, he'll make me watch." She searched his eyes. "It'll be worse if he knows you're my mate."

"Well, we won't let him notice, then!" he snapped stubbornly.

"Maybe he will mention Fern..." Raphael growled and his eyes flashed amber at her words. Artemis grimaced before looking at him pointedly.

"Ah, fuck!" Moving away from her, Raphael scrubbed his hands over his face before linking his fingers on top of his head. "Fuck! Fuck! Fuck!" he spat angrily.

"You should be sleeping. Go rest a bit more." She pulled on his hand, but he only pulled harder and wrapped her in an embrace while burying his head in her neck. "I'll think of something." She pressed closer to him holding him tight.

"My entire family was slaughtered because I was not capable of helping." His words took her off guard as she pulled back to look at him. "The night I met my maker, my family died because of me. I was human and couldn't do anything to help them. I vowed it would never happen again. That's why I never cared about anyone or got attached. So I never have to feel that hopelessness again." His eyes shimmered as he looked away as if ashamed. It broke her heart to see him like that. "Until now!" He looked back at her. "I will not stand back and hope that you will be fine!"

Artemis looked at him for long moments. She had bottled down all of her emotions, apart from anger, most of her life because she didn't want to feel what he had just described. She knew it took a lot for someone like Raphael to speak out loud about weaknesses, and she admired him for his courage. A lump clogged her throat, but she kept her face stoic, not wanting to anger him or disrespect him by showing pity. He didn't need her to pity him. He needed her to show him enough trust and respect and find a solution together.

"I have been fighting this battle on my own, my whole life, Raphael. Forgive me if I don't know how to do this as a team." His eyes softened and she embraced him again "We will do this together. I just hope we survive it," she whispered in his ear.

Chapter Thirty-Two

Iris was surprised to see Artemis and Raphael walk through the door of her ritual room. She frowned as she looked at the vampire, who should be dead for the world for another six hours, minimum. Artemis had a determined look on her face as she pulled on the shirt Iris gave her to wear. The Fae was not used to human clothing, so she scratched and picked on it constantly, making Iris feel bad that she had nothing else to offer her. Dresses were out of the question if they wanted Raphael to stay focused.

"Something is the matter, witch?" Stopping where Iris was kneeling on the floor tracing sigils with salt trickling from her hand, he narrowed his eyes. "You look like I killed your pet."

"Why are you awake?" Iris blurted.

"That's what I asked as well, but got no answer," Artemis told Iris before she turned to look at Raphael with her eyebrow raised. "He always distracts me when I ask a question he doesn't want to answer."

"I'm assuming it's because of the bond." A line formed between his brows as he looked from Artemis to Iris and back. "Or the Fae blood. And, it's a pointless conversation. I'm good to go and I'm not complaining. Anything that gives us the advantage, I'm happy with."

"We need to know what else has changed. It might have unwanted side effects, you know," Iris pointed out, making Raphael fume.

"Nothing about her or from her is unwanted, witch! I ignore most of your ramblings, but don't push your luck. Not with this!" he snapped at her, making her recoil.

"She didn't mean it the way you took it, Raphael. Calm down!" Artemis gripped his arm, and it was physically evident how his body reacted to and relaxed at her touch. "Does this mean that sunlight doesn't affect you anymore? We need to know before you set foot on the other side. Or wait until nightfall when your strength is at full force."

"We need to walk around the realm? I thought we are just retrieving your weapon this time." He placed his hand over hers on his arm when she tried to pull it away. "Is there something you're not telling me?"

"I just worry, that's all." She shook her head as if his words were disappointing. "Just like you, I'd rather not take chances with your life. We don't know what will happen when we go through."

"We'll be fine!" He straightened his shoulders.

Artemis wished she had the same confidence as he did. It was crippling to feel this fear for another. A nagging feeling in her stomach was telling her that things would go wrong no matter how much she tried to stay in control of the situation. Their only hope was that Lazarus was not expecting them. If they managed to get in and out, they'd have more time to come up with a plan on how to fix this. At the moment she needed to focus and not fight the insistent pull she felt from it. She hadn't said a word because Raphael would go ballistic and plow through the portal without reason, getting himself killed. Summoning all her confidence, she looked down as Iris traced the last line of the sigil.

"Let's do this as soon as Iris is ready." Faking a reassuring smile, she turned to Raphael, "Do you have my arrow? You should leave it with Iris so she can pull me back here if things don't go as planned. Even if I get captured by my father, the arrow will pull me through. I won't fight it."

"It's in the car. I'll go get it, with my speed the sunlight won't hurt me in such short time." Kissing Artemis's forehead, he strutted out of the room before she can protest.

As soon as she couldn't hear him, Artemis turned to Iris. "If you have a feeling something is wrong, I need you to pull him out of there! Do you hear me?" Artemis looked at the witch intently.

"He'll kill me! Are you insane?" Iris hissed back, keeping her voice low in fear he might hear her.

"I will hunt you down and you'll wish someone had killed you first if anything happens to him that you could've stopped!" Artemis snapped as her eyes flashed, their glow as eerie as it was beautiful to watch.

Inhaling a shaky breath, with no other option but to agree, Iris nodded jerkily. She was still looking at Artemis when Raphael walked back in, holding the arrow in a tight grip. His eyes narrowed when he saw them locked in a staring match. Iris smiled at him tightly before lifting herself off the ground and dusting her hands of the grains of salt still stuck to her palms.

"Why do I have a feeling that I was sent out of here so you two could plot something?" He kept looking from one woman to the other.

"Because you're a vampire who thinks everyone is like you, and because you're paranoid!" Iris told him, irritated. "I'm more worried about your buddy deciding to come visit while you two aren't here. I don't buy his bullshit that he doesn't remember anything."

"He won't!" Raphael smiled grimly at her. "It'll take him finding a way out first. And that, witch," he pointed a finger at her, "won't happen. You can bet your life on it."

"Well, I kinda am betting it, you jackass!" she snapped before closing her eyes and inhaling deeply. "Sorry. I'm just freaked out, that's all."

"In and out, Iris." Artemis walked up to the witch and grabbed her shoulders. "We will be back before you know it, I promise." The look Artemis gave her had more meaning than the words she spoke, so Iris nodded slowly, letting Artemis know that she'd gotten the message loud and clear.

Stepping away, Iris lifted her hands and stretched out her fingers, wiggling them. Her breath whistled through the air as she exhaled through pursed lips before walking around and sitting on her haunches at the top of her intricate circle. Closing her eyes, she started humming, and it grew in volume while her fingers kept making that pattern that Raphael kept meaning to ask about. Artemis wiped her palms off on the pants Iris had given her, preparing herself for whatever came their way. Raphael leaned down, dropping the arrow on the floor close to Iris before straightening up and balling his fists. This was it! His first travel to a different realm and it was as exciting as it was terrifying. He just had to stay focused and not make things more difficult with the temper he'd developed since he met his mate. *Fuck me! I better be able to do this,* his mind screamed at him. *I can do this!* he thought sternly. As he watched the colors start popping and swirling in the middle of the witch's circle, he was almost certain he could. *Kinda!* his mind supplied helpfully.

Chapter Thirty-Three

Artemis glanced once at Iris, making sure the witch was fine and could handle herself before squaring her shoulders and walking through the opened portal with Raphael right on her heels. She wasn't sure what she was expecting to see, but it wasn't the empty portal room or the deathly silence that surrounded her. Raphael's warm palm on her back was as welcome as it was distracting. She looked at him over her shoulder and smiled tightly before taking a deep breath and trying to locate her weapon. It called to her no matter where she was.

"Stay close and quiet," she said very softly, knowing that he would hear her perfectly.

On silent feet she walked to the entrance, stopping only to glance out really quickly, assuring herself that there was no one in the hallway before walking out like she owned the palace. There was no one around. Not the gossipers, not a stray person going somewhere. It looked like the place was deserted. Her stomach was in knots and the anxiety was eating at her. Something was very wrong, and it had nothing to do with her disappearance. No one cared a great deal about her, she knew that much.

"I've never been here before, but even I feel that something is wrong." Raphael's words were spoken softly, for her ears only. Glancing back at him, she nodded and continued to follow the pull she felt in her chest.

The uneasiness Artemis felt grew exponentially when she was led to her father's wing. The large hallway was as empty as the rest of the palace... as quiet as a tomb. Her nerves prickled with the feeling that she was being watched just as the hand Raphael held at constant contact with her back gripped her shirt tightly. He felt it too, she knew it. Not wanting to alert whoever was watching them that she was aware, she kept a steady gait and kept walking. The decorative pieces and art on the walls were blurry as she ignored everything but reaching the massive double doors in front of her. If she could get her weapon, they would be fine.

Raphael was trying his best to keep a leash on his instincts screaming at him to protect his mate. He gripped her shirt so tightly in his fist he was surprised the fabric didn't rip. It felt like his fingers had fused together and he couldn't release it if he tried. Everywhere he turned, bright colors met his gaze. This realm was so much more vivid and so colorful that his eyes stung as he squinted in an effort to see better. For a split second his mind wondered how earth looked to Artemis. Did it seem so drab, so washed out that she wouldn't want to stay there with him? He pushed that thought to the back of his mind. *Focus!* he berated himself.

The closer they got to the doors, the more Raphael could feel Artemis stiffening under his fisted hand. On the outside, she looked like she was walking with purpose, not batting an eye. He could feel her anxiety through their bond, though, making his own skyrocket. Both of them slowed down, then stopped as a light breeze ruffled their hair and made goosebumps cover Artemis all over. She didn't dare move her eyes from the closed doors while Raphael looked around them with a scowl on his face. Everything around Artemis started fading into shadow as the doors got brighter. She felt her body coiling to spring from where she stood in the hope that she would get there in time.

Her eyes locked on the intricate gold doorknob that started moving painfully slowly. Her heart leaped into her throat as a door opened to their left. Neither she nor Raphael had time to react as Raphael was snatched away from her, ripping her shirt in the process and leaving it to hang in tatters on her shoulders before he was shoved into the room. Ivy, her father's consort, grabbed her under her arm, almost digging fingernails into her skin just as the door in front of her opened and Lazarus filled the doorway.

"Oh, thank the fates you're here!" Ivy exclaimed, and when Artemis looked at her, she realized Ivy was talking to her father. "She's back!" she gushed, acting like a worried mother and utterly confusing Artemis. "And she's alive!" Ivy continued, pulling Artemis along as she started walking.

On wooden legs and with a numb mind, Artemis allowed herself to be pulled forward as her eyes locked with the cold green ones in her father's face. There was something there, like he was mocking her, internally laughing at her, that rubbed her the wrong way, and she glared at him. Her own eyes must have betrayed her, because his wings unfurled and he stepped away from the doorway as if ready for a fight. Ivy's nails dug deeper into her skin, taking her focus away from Lazarus. Who knew the woman had daggers for nails? Artemis felt the drip of her blood gliding on her skin and her insides clenched. *Raphael!* her mind screamed at her, but she had to stay alive to go after him. Artemis knew two things for sure. One, he was alive, albeit angrier than ever. Two, Ivy was next to her, and if anything happened to him, Ivy would wish and pray for death.

"Where were you?" The deep voice of Lazarus broke through her internal panic. His wings were spread out, almost blocking half the doors behind him.

"I was trapped and held captive," Artemis said calmly, surprising herself. "I escaped." Her voice sounded hollow to her own ears.

"Just like that." Lazarus narrowed his eyes and he clenched his fists as he took a step towards her.

"She's alive, I think that…"

"No one cares what you think!" Lazarus snapped at Ivy, cutting her off.

"No, not just like that," Artemis spoke loudly enough to get his attention off Ivy. "I had to kill quite a few of them, but it made things fun," she continued conversationally, shrugging a shoulder. "The important thing is that I'm back!" Lifting her chin, she glared, daring him to say something.

"Yes, I see you are," Lazarus mused. "And right on time, too!"

"On time for what? My own search party?" Artemis tried for humor, but her words sounded accusatory. The cruel smile lifting the corners of her father's lips was like a knife in her gut.

"Let us not wait, since you are so curious, daughter." He came at her with long strides, grabbing her free arm and almost dragging her along with him. "Let me show you!"

Looking over her shoulder, Artemis glanced desperately at the closed door where she hoped Raphael was and then at Ivy. The color had drained from the other woman's face, but she gave Artemis an encouraging nod as if reading her mind. If this was how it felt to worry about a mate, Artemis needed to find and kill the fates. This crippling fear was something she wouldn't wish on her worst enemy. Not even on Lazarus.

Chapter Thirty-Four

Raphael felt out of his mind when he was pulled harshly into a room and the door was slammed in his face. All the panic he felt from Artemis, coupled with his fear for her life, made him go ballistic. He wasn't sure how long he'd been throwing his entire body at the door, yanking on it with all the strength he had, with no effect. Nothing would budge. It was as if the whole place was made out of some material that made him more useless than a human.

Looking down at his feet, he saw a piece of Artemis's shirt that he must have ripped off when he'd been pulled away. Scooping it up, he brought it to his nose and inhaled deeply. Her scent, like fresh air in a dark tomb, calmed him down... a little. Long enough that he felt certain that she was alive, anyway. Her fear, anger and anxiety mixed tighter, and he felt it all as if it were his own. That made him stop and think. If he let it overwhelm him, both of them might not leave this realm. He needed to find a way out of this room and to find her.

Raphael knew when she was walking away, and it felt

like she was yanking at a rope tied to the center of his chest as she was gaining distance. With no other options left, he walked calmly to the door and tried the doorknob as if everything in the world was right. It didn't open, naturally, and he shook his head at himself.

"That almost looked civil." A deep male voice spoke behind him, making Raphael whirl around, baring his fangs and snarling. "Well, I did say *almost* civil." A tall blue-eyed male was perched on the edge of a large bed, his arms crossed.

"Who the fuck are you?" Raphael got in his face. "Open this damn door!"

"And you'll go where, exactly?" Snorting, the male didn't even blink at the angry vampire whose fangs were gleaming, ready to rip him to shreds.

Raphael had enough of bullshit and grabbed for the male, but stopped and frowned when his hands passed through the male like he wasn't there. This room was getting crazier by the second, and he had just about had enough of it. His instincts were screaming at him to kill the male and go find his mate, but all he could do about it was fume, snarl and nothing else. Stopping his panting and snarling, Raphael pinched the bridge of his nose before rubbing a hand over his face. At least he was grateful that the headaches had stopped.

"You're a fucking ghost!" Raphael mumbled with his eyes closed as his nostrils flared while he tried to calm himself down. "That's all I needed right now. A ghost!"

"First of all, I'm not a ghost!" Smirking, the male stood up. He was as tall as Raphael but leaner, with long black hair falling over his shoulders. "Ivy is a seer, and she can also walk the ether. She pulled me here, so I'm not stuck in my body or in that ghostly place." Raphael was getting more confused by the second. "My name is Fern, by the way."

At hearing the name, Raphael attacked again, but he only managed to go through Fern and stumble over the bed. Snarling, he tried again a few more times before stopping, though he continued glaring at Fern.

"You must've heard of me," Fern chuckled as amusement danced in his eyes.

"You can't be here! You're in my realm with Iris." Raphael spat at him and immediately felt stupid for even having the conversation. "While Artemis is out there alone and I'm stuck here with you!"

"Artemis will be fine. You forget she's a warrior and much stronger than any of us here. I'm not sure even Lazarus can compare. Why do you think he had her on a short leash?" Fern tried to calm Raphael down but only made him angry.

"Watch your mouth, Fae!" There was so much malice in Raphael's words that Fern's hairs stood on end.

"Listen! I get it! I had enough time to listen to Ivy as she went on and on about everything that she's seen in her dreams to know who and what you are, as well as knowing that you're the only hope Artemis has to stay alive. I was crazier than you the first time I showed up in this room and couldn't touch anything." Fern glared at him.

"What?" Raphael forgot how to breathe at hearing Fern's words. "What did you just say?"

Fern went on full alert, stiffening up even though he knew the vampire couldn't touch him. Instincts were stronger than reason. Raphael's quiet and deceptively calm voice made alarms scream in Fern's head to get the hell away from him. Unfortunately for both of them, they were stuck here together.

"It would better if Ivy told you. I don't remember all the details." Fern kept watching the vampire warily. "That woman has gotten me into more trouble than I care to admit, but looking back now, I see that it all had to pass to stop this insanity that will destroy us all. I just know that you need to be here at this moment. When it's time, she will come to get you, I'm sure." He frowned as if he couldn't believe his own words.

"She's in danger because of me," Raphael told him as if they were having a friendly conversation. "I need to find a way to get out of this room."

"Well, we're both out of luck. I have no idea how Ivy does half of the things she does, and it's even unfathomable to me to think that Lazarus doesn't know about it. But from what I've seen the last few days I've been stuck here, I think we should trust her."

"You can trust whomever you want. I'm out of here!" Raphael growled as he turned towards the door, eyeing it.

"Don't be so stubborn, you'll only exhaust yourself. Keep your strength, because you'll need it," Fern told him conversationally. "Ivy saw all possible paths, and the one that was most promising for all of us to stay alive is the one she made sure would come to pass." Lifting a hand to stop any rebuttal, he shook his head. "Don't ask me how! I stopped questioning it. She told me the exact moment you and Artemis would be walking past that door. She waited to pull you in so Lazarus wouldn't see you. If that's not enough proof, I don't know what else to say."

"You don't like him." Raphael looked at Fern with narrowed eyes.

"Only a fool would like that monster. I did many wrongs when I trusted him!" Fern spat angrily. "He lied to all of us and we followed him like fools. The realm is dying because of him, and soon all of us will be gone because of his greed for power. He killed Artemis's mother to take the throne, but he failed." A brief, wry laugh escaped his lips. "She was too smart for the likes of him. She hid it, and no one can find that throne room. The Obsidian Throne is lost to us, but he made his own. He'll be the death of all of us if we don't stop him, mark my words."

Raphael's mind was spinning. It sounded like Claude was telling the truth after all. Well, part of it, at least. And if Lazarus had no problem killing the mother, he probably wouldn't bat an eye at killing the daughter. Urgency pulled at him, but he knew he had to wait.

"Why hide the throne?" Raphael asked just to keep himself busy and not go insane.

"That throne unites the light and the dark or destroys it all, depending on who's sitting on it. From what I've heard, it's waiting for someone. When the queen hid it, she made sure that the right person would find it."

"A warrior with a bleeding heart," Raphael mumbled under his breath, remembering Claude's words.

"You know about it?" Fern looks at him incredulously.

"I heard about that yesterday. Apparently my maker was aware of it." He gave Fern a humorless smile. "And was very much aware of Lazarus, if Claude is to be believed."

"Well, I have no idea who Claude is, but I do know that only one that has compassion and a pure heart can find it."

"Good luck finding that amongst our kinds." Raphael laughed, surprising himself. Fern smiled slightly at that. "And stay away from Artemis, she's mine! If you need the motivation to keep your distance, remember that I know where your physical body is. You'll stay a ghost forever!"

"Ivy told me." Lifting both hands in surrender, Fern's eyes widened. "She's all yours. I don't get between mates."

Raphael opened his mouth to say more, but the door unlocked so suddenly that even Fern jumped up and bent his knees into a fighting stance. They had no time to look at the woman properly as she ran towards Raphael, grabbing him by the hand and dragging him with her. Her silver hair flew around and she looked like she glowed, but Raphael was too alert for any possible for danger to make sure he saw things that didn't matter.

"We have to hurry!" Her musical voice floated as she bolted through the hallways with Raphael hard on her heels.

"That's Ivy!" Fern yelled, and his voice followed Raphael from the room.

Chapter Thirty-Five

Artemis stood frozen, forgetting how to breathe when Lazarus dragged her outside of the palace. The beautiful nature that she loved so much was gone. Everywhere she looked, there was only grayness and destruction. Where once ancient trees stood, now only dead trunks with no leaves pointed at the sky, as if reaching for help that wasn't coming. The beautiful colors that her home had been known for were gone. What stood in their place were rows and rows of armored Fae looking straight at her, making her want to unleash her fury on them. But it wasn't their fault. No! It was the one standing next to her, his eyes glowing proudly as he looked at everything that he'd destroyed.

"What happened in the few days I was gone?" Not looking at Lazarus, Artemis kept glancing around, blinking rapidly, in hopes that the scenery would change. It stayed the same.

"Sometimes, my daughter, we must sacrifice one thing to achieve another." Lazarus spoke loudly, making everyone as far as her eyes could see shout their salute. Bile rose in her throat. "No price is too high to reach a goal," he murmured for her ears only. "Most of them will die." Looking at her and smiling as if he wanted her to be happy with that revelation he kept talking, and each word felt like a dagger in her heart. "But they don't need to know that. What they need to know is that they're dying for the greater good!"

"Whose greater good?" Artemis asked through numb lips. *I helped him do this!* her mind screamed so loudly she almost staggered.

"Ours, of course!" Lazarus scoffed as if she were slow for not seeing it until now.

"Remind me again, father." She turned her head slowly towards him. "Why exactly are we doing this?"

"To avenge your mother and keep that portal open." He spat angrily. "They killed my love and banished us from their realm! We need that portal open to keep thriving."

"That's not what the vampire king said," Artemis told him calmly, watching his reaction.

Lazarus stiffened and slowly turned his entire body towards her. His eyes turned flat and cold as his lips twisted in a sneer, making her fight her instincts to accept the challenge that he gave and attack him.

"You would believe your mother's killers over your own blood?" He roared in her face, all pretense of calm gone.

"It was a simple statement," she told him calmly, while wondering how she managed to do it when her entire body and soul were screaming at her to kill him. "Every story has two sides, does it not?"

"You know nothing!" Sneering, he got in her face, but Artemis stood her ground. Luckily Ivy had disappeared somewhere, so Artemis didn't have to worry about her getting caught in the middle of a fight. "I can smell those useless rodents all over you! Is that all it took? A few days to turn you against your own?"

"No one turned anyone against their own. I just want to know the truth!" Lifting her chin, she looked at him defiantly, not backing down.

"You know the truth!" His voice carried as he practically screamed in her face, and the troops were starting to get restless uncertain of what was going on.

"Do I?" Lifting her eyebrow, a calm enveloped her out of nowhere. This was the moment of truth, and she knew it to her bones. "Do I really know the truth...father?" She tilted her head, watching him.

Lazarus was not looking at her eyes or her face. His entire focus was aimed at her neck, and it took her a long moment to realize what he saw there. The marks from Raphael's fangs were still visible on her skin, and she almost pushed them in her father's face so he could see them.

"So you're a vampire whore, just like your mother was!"

Artemis felt faint at hearing his words. There was no anger in them. No, there was a promise of pain and death as Lazarus slowly spread his wings and his power slammed into her chest, almost making her take a step back. An eerie silence surrounded them at his words, and Lazarus slowly turned his head to look at the Fae that just like Artemis, stood frozen in place.

"Yes! You heard me right! Your queen was a vampire whore, letting filthy bloodsuckers into her body and giving them her lifeblood!" he roared.

"You killed her!" Artemis growled loud enough that it felt like the realm was holding its breath to hear the answer.

"I did not kill a queen! I killed a whore!" At his words, the shouts and yells were deafening. Yet Lazarus kept looking at her with a crazed look in his eyes, his face ugly in its beauty with a sneer on it.

Artemis looked at him for a long moment as her chest kept rising and falling faster with each breath she took. She felt his admission as a hot poker in her heart, and her entire life flashed before her eyes. All the times she'd been punished as he watched with glee, not once caring if her blood was spilled or her bones were broken. Tough love, he called it, but now she knew. Lazarus knew it, too, because his eyes flashed with triumph at her realization. A cold smile blossomed on his face while Artemis was fighting not to go feral and truly become the monster he wanted her to be by killing everyone.

"You are not my father." Her words were almost a whisper as his smile grew.

"Aww," he mocked her. "Are you disappointed, Artemis? I know I would be," he gloated, while pain seared her insides.

Movement caught her eye at the doors, and she knew that Raphael had managed to find her. She clenched her teeth as rage overtook reason. If anyone could bring her back from the brink, it was Raphael. He would not let her kill innocents, she knew that much. This time her lips started lifting at the corners slowly, and Lazarus first looked confused, then frowned. Her smile grew as he sneered and launched for her, but she moved away faster and stayed out of his reach. She glanced at Raphael, and he nodded at her. He knew what she was planning, feeling it through their bond. That was all she needed to know before following her instincts, and her body shifted into her other form. She smiled wickedly, looking down at Lazarus.

"This is the day you die!"

Chapter Thirty-Six

Raphael watched the exchange between Artemis and Lazarus with such focus that the roars from the crowd of armored Fae made his head go numb from shock. Fear for Artemis made his body coil up, ready to protect her, but he should've known better. No matter how much his instincts were telling him to stand like a shield in front of the one that was part of his soul, she was a predator herself—a killer he had feared not long ago but now looked at with pride welling up in his chest. Artemis didn't need him to protect her. She needed him to watch her back, and that was precisely what he was going to do. Just like she told him, they were a team now. He felt more confident as he watched more than half the Fae separate from the whole and point their glowing weapons towards those that cheered Lazarus.

Black wings spread out and hid Artemis from Raphael's view for a second before Lazarus rose up in the air, looking like a fallen angel from lore. His black hair was blowing around his face as his eyes glowed like lanterns. Shadows burst from his body, surrounding him like a shield. The grayness stretched and twisted like a living thing, jerking its tentacles towards Artemis as if trying to pull her close. Raphael clenched his fists, preparing to lunge at it himself when a hand gripped his forearm, yanking him back. He snarled in Ivy's face, long thick fangs chomping an inch from it and making her recoil.

"You will get her killed if she has to think about keeping you safe while she's fighting Lazarus! Don't be insane!" Ivy hissed at him.

"You expect me to hide like a coward and watch?" Snapping at her, Raphael jerked his arm trying to dislodge her grip, but Ivy held onto it stubbornly. The woman was much stronger than she looked with her golden glow and porcelain skin.

"Don't be stupid, bloodsucker! She is the strongest amongst us! You, on the other hand, don't stand a chance. Watch!" She lifted her chin and with her free hand, pointed behind him.

Artemis stood proudly, clutching her bow in her hand, and watched Lazarus release the hold on his powers. They were so different from her own that it produced the feeling that they glided over each other like oil and water, touching but not mixing at all. When his wings stretched out and he lifted off the ground, she smiled at him. It was the first honest smile she had given him. Finally there would be an end to the madness and she could face her foe—the one that Artemis had been searching for her whole life but was right before her eyes. The shadows around Lazarus started lashing out, trying to grab hold of her, and her wings fluttered, preparing to get out of their way if needed. The sounds of weapons clashing, yells and roars started fading slowly. Everything around her disappeared, and all she could see was Lazarus.

"So, you like everyone to see you die a coward?" Lazarus boomed, pulling a sword out of thin air.

"Less talking, more fighting." She grinned at him; more a baring of teeth than an actual smile.

Lazarus twirled the long thin sword few times around his hand before launching himself at her. Artemis was expecting him to try to take her off guard, so she twisted around as the glowing blade missed her by an inch. She felt the heat of it on her skin and watched a lock of her hair float to the ground. Lazarus had a crazed look in his eyes as he smiled at her in triumph. That was too close to her liking. She flicked her tail with as much strength as she could muster, catching him off guard and flinging him higher in the air. His wings closed in around him, making him look like a ball of feathers flying up in the air before he opened them up and plunged down towards her like a bullet.

Artemis allowed her wings to bring her down. Her body was larger than his, making him faster in the air. He tried to force her to fight that way, hoping to use it in his advantage, but she stayed calm and deflected all his blows. She needed to bide her time and wait for the chance to get him at just the right moment. It bothered her to play the weakling, but there was something about those shadows and that blade that wasn't sitting well with her.

Lazarus was getting overconfident in his attempts to get Artemis into the air. *Maybe the bloodsuckers have hurt her, and she wasn't healed yet,* he thought as he watched her get back on the ground again. He was frustrated that she wasn't fighting, only fending off his attempts to push the blade into her soft flesh. He should've done it before she shifted, but he was confident he would get his chance soon. She seemed mellow, not the vicious killer he spent his life creating. He lunged at her again, this time slicing her arm above the elbow. The shadows floating around him wrapped around her form, feeding off her life force and becoming darker in color from it. His laughter boomed and was heard over the sounds of fighting as her blood dripped from his blade, down her arm.

Artemis didn't feel pain. She felt the blade split her skin like it was a silk scarf gliding over it. The warmth of her blood was telling her that her skin was chilled and she frowned as she watched the red run down her arm in rivulets. *What a strange feeling...* she thought a second before she saw the shadows pulling on her energy like leeches would suck blood. She flung her body away from them lifting up in the air as shivers ran down her spine. Her eyes jerked up from her arm when a roar so loud it shook the ground echoed around her. It silenced everything like it had frozen everyone in place a second before a large body jumped high into the air from the doors and like a cannonball, collided with Lazarus, both of them dropping to the ground in a tangled mess of limbs and wings.

Fear made Artemis forget all about her plans to wait for the perfect opportunity to kill Lazarus. As she watched Raphael pin Lazarus on the ground, holding him down between his powerful thighs, her heart stopped beating for long moments before starting back up again so fast that she felt dizzy. Throwing herself in their direction, she had just enough time to see Lazarus smile like he had already won before the glowing blade disappeared between the two men and her body collided with Raphael's, sending them both rolling away from Lazarus. Her blood turned to ice when she heard Lazarus laugh out loud as her body shifted to its human form.

Chapter Thirty-Seven

"Oh, how tragic! You brought one of them here!" Lifting himself up Lazarus kept laughing.

Artemis ignored him and everything else as she rolled Raphael onto his back. There was an anguished scream that echoed for what felt like an eternity, blanketing everything around them in silence, almost like the realm itself held its breath. She stopped breathing as her eyes connected with his. There was an apology clear in Raphael's green eyes looking at her face as if he was trying to memorize it. Her hands pressed at the gaping hole in his chest where blood was pulsing out of it with each pump of his heart. Artemis was pushing as hard as she could, but it kept seeping through her fingers, soaking his shirt.

"Don't you dare die!" she snapped at him, fear making her angry. "How dare you come into my life to just walk out of it like this!"

Raphael lifted his hand, cupping her face, and parted his lips as if to say something. She was so focused on him, his mussed hair sticking to his forehead, the painfully beautiful face with its high cheekbones and square jaw, that no sound penetrated the grief that overwhelmed her. That was until Raphael's green eyes widened, the long thick lashes framing them stopped fluttering when he looked over her shoulder a second before she felt the hot metal blade pressed firmly to her neck.

"History always repeats itself, you know." Lazarus spoke from behind her, digging the sword deeper into her skin. "Like mother, like daughter." He sounded disappointed, making Artemis want to puke, "This is also how she died, you know? Protecting the filth!" Lazarus spat.

Raphael struggled under her palms, trying to lift himself up while panic and helplessness were making him stare at her as if no matter what was going on around them, he didn't want to lose one precious second of looking at her face. Artemis ignored the searing pain and the feel of the blood sliding down like the tears that for the first time trickled down her face. It took her a moment to realize what the wetness was as her vision blurred and cleared in rapid succession. Raphael's eyes filled up as well as they followed each drop sliding down her cheek.

Lazarus kept talking, but no one paid attention to his words. The fighting had stopped at Artemis's scream, and all eyes were turned on them. It was the moment Lazarus had lived for. To be the center of attention, to have everyone witness his power and never question his position. This whole situation was turning out better than he could've hoped for. He would never admit it, not even in his own mind, but he feared that Artemis might end him eventually. Keeping her weakened by making her fight in the arena was one way that Lazarus had made sure to keep her in check. Now the stupid bloodsucker gave him the greatest gift of all.

Her head! With a gleam in his glowing eyes, he started lifting the sword up in the air.

"Fight!" Raphael wheezed, unable to speak above a whisper from the pain in his chest. His insides felt as though they were burning, as if he'd swallowed the sun and it was turning him to ashes from the inside out. "Please! I want you to live! For me!"

Pain. That's what Artemis felt as it overtook her entire being. Grief for her mother, for Raphael, for Fern too, no matter how much he deserved what happened to him when he broke the oath. Even for Ivy, who for some reason had also helped her when Artemis had been sure that the other woman didn't even like her. She felt the pain of her home as well. The realm that had somehow started dying in the few days she'd been gone and now looked more like the pits of hell than the heavenly beauty she remembered.

It was all Lazarus's fault. The evil radiating from him was unmistakable. Her body stiffened and shifted. Her tail lashed out behind her, sending Lazarus flying back, slamming into the walls of the palace. Bricks crumbled as he went through them, making a hole in the wall big enough for Artemis to walk through in her shifted form. She was done waiting for the right moment. She had nothing left to lose.

Ivy came running from the palace doors and dropped to her knees next to Raphael. Artemis reached down to grab her and fling her away, but the other woman lifted the bow and arrows, handing them to her.

"Go! I'll do what I can to try to save him! Go kill that monster!" Ivy pushed the bow higher, and as soon as Artemis snatched it, she turned to Raphael. "Stupid vampire. I told you to trust her and wait!" she mumbled at him as Artemis watched the golden glow start to flow from

Ivy's hands into Raphael's chest. Ivy looked up, frowning. "Go! What are you waiting for?"

"If he dies..." Artemis growled, making Ivy's skin pebble with goosebumps.

"Yeah, yeah, I know. You'll find me, kill me, blah, blah...Go! I'll do everything I can to keep him alive!" With a tight nod to Ivy, Artemis turned around and advanced on the hole in the wall.

Stepping through the ruined wall, she had to slightly bend her head as her entire shifted body passed through. Slinging her quiver over her shoulder, Artemis pulled an arrow out and nocked it. Her eyes searched around, seeing overturned cots, chairs and tables as well as the few weapons leaning on the far side wall. An off-duty guard room, most likely. The open door got her attention, and her eyes started glowing in the dimly lit place. The hunt called to her nature.

"Hey, Lazarus!" she called out loud enough that even those fighting outside could hear her words as they echoed off the walls as she headed out to look for him. "Where did you go? We have unfinished business to discuss!"

She heard sounds from up ahead, like the dragging of feet and bumping into things. Her smile turned feral. Excitement pumped through her veins as the evil surrounding Lazarus swirled in the air like a trail of smoke left behind him, pointing in his direction like a glowing sign. Artemis chuckled as her six legs started finding holds between bricks and her body was lifted off the ground. She climbed the walls, scurrying ahead, following her prey. She was bloodthirsty, and only one creature could quench her thirst. She just had to find him.

Chapter Thirty-Eight

The deserted hallways looked like they were shrinking as Artemis crawled the walls and ceilings, following the trail of shadows Lazarus was leaving behind. It occurred to her that it might be a trap and that he was leading her to where he wanted her, but at the moment she was willing to follow him to her death, just to get her hands on him. The colors around her seemed brighter, almost like every object she passed radiated a life of its own. As the shadowed trail got thicker, the life glowing from everything around her got muted. She realized that the shadow was feeding off the bright glow around her.

Reaching the wide winding stairways, she scurried faster toward the upper floors and with a sharp left turn, headed towards Lazarus's rooms. Of course he would hide there. Who knew what he had hidden in those rooms that no one was allowed to enter? Even his consort was not allowed there; Ivy's rooms were next to his, but she never set foot there. Slowing down, she crept up slowly towards the closed double doors that in her shifted form appeared warded. A red glow, like a border, surrounded them, pulsing like a wall of fire. Getting as close as she could, Artemis stopped debating her options. If she knew Lazarus at all, he would expect her to go barging in straight through those doors.

"Artemis!" The hissing whisper got her to lash out with her tail on reflex, almost breaking the partially-open door behind her. So much for subtlety.

Narrowing her eyes, she slowly crept towards it, gripping one arrow in her hand. She was aware that she couldn't walk through that door in the form she was in. Her body was too large. Gripping the doorframe with all her legs, she extended her torso through the door carefully. Artemis wasn't sure what she had expected, but seeing Fern shimmering like a ghost in the middle of the room with his arms crossed was definitely not it.

"Shift back and come in, please!" Fern spoke softly although his face showed the impatience he felt. "I'm stuck in this stupid room and can't do shit right now!"

Artemis looked around the room carefully, wondering if it was some trick Lazarus was pulling to get her to shift back to her human form. Nothing would surprise her coming from him. She glared at Fern while weighing her options—ignore him and go to the doors to reach Lazarus, or see what was going on with Fern first.

"It's not a trick, Ivy pulled me here. I know my body is in the human realm." Fern rolled his eyes as Artemis's glare intensified. "Your mate said my body is with Iris, whoever she may be," he supplied helpfully.

At hearing the name and the mention of her mate, Artemis shifted back to her human form, dropping lightly on the balls of her feet. Slipping inside the room, she closed the door behind her but didn't step closer to where Fern stood. He hadn't moved an inch.

"What's going on?" she growled, still holding the arrow in her fist. "How are you here?"

"Did you know Ivy was a seer as well as a dreamweaver?" Fern's question made her look at him incredulously. "Yeah, neither did I!" he grimaced. "That woman is playing some dangerous games, I can tell you that much."

"What kind of a games?" Her chest was rising and falling faster. Urgency was pulling her to go finish what she'd started with Lazarus, but she also needed to know if leaving Raphael with Ivy was the worst decision she has made.

"I think everything we know about Ivy is a carefully crafted façade. She's a seer, that much I know for sure. She told me everything about what you'll be going through in the human realm. Including finding your mate when no Fae has found a mate for centuries."

"That doesn't tell me much!" Artemis waved him away. "She could be cunning enough to have spies in the human realm following us around if we cross the portal."

"She helped me walk through the portal so I could talk to the witch. I was told I must do that if we're all to survive what's coming. Forgive me if doing what felt right was inconveniencing you, your majesty!" He glared, daring her to say something. "Ivy knew the exact moment you would be walking past this door with your mate and she knew she had to pull him into this room so Lazarus wouldn't see him." Fern lifted his chin stubbornly, reminding her how much he hated it when she doubted him.

"For what reason? What's in this for her? No one here does anything just for the sake of helping, Fern. Including you!" she pointed the arrow at him, but seeing him shimmer made her realize how stupid that was and she lowered it.

"Whatever her reasons, she hates Lazarus as much as you...if not more. That should be enough for now," he persisted.

"And you're here how? And why?"

"The oath I gave to keep the secrets Lazarus showed me almost killed me. I don't know who Iris is..."

"She's the witch that you got cozy with. A changeling, to be more precise," Artemis supplied, cutting him off. Fern glared at her, so she rolled her eyes and motioned for him to continue.

"As I was saying,"—he cleared his throat—"Whoever it was, they managed to hold me frozen in the state I was in. I cannot express the pain in words. Then this light showed up in the darkness that wrapped around me like a blanket. It took the pain away and started pulling me towards a door. I was so grateful for the agony to end that I would've followed the devil himself anywhere. When I opened my eyes, I was standing in this room, like a ghost, and Ivy was standing in front of me. I was in this state... I don't even know what to call it. That's when she told me that she's a seer and she knew all of this would happen. She was ready to help us, to make sure Lazarus was no more."

Artemis listened to his every word and felt uneasy about this whole revelation. But thinking about it now, what choice did they have? Ivy had better keep her promise for Raphael to be alive. If not, she would beg for a death that will never come. Beggars can't be choosers at the moment, so she was willing to let things slide and not look at the gift for faults.

"Now what?" Artemis searched his eyes. "You stopped me from getting to Lazarus so I could hear the story of how poor Ivy was a nice woman and she tried to help?"

"You can be such a bitch!" Fern hissed, clenching his fists at his sides. "I stopped you so you wouldn't fry yourself when you tried to walk through those doors!" He flung his hand towards the doors to Lazarus's rooms. "He warded those doors especially against you!"

"So how do I get in?" Her heart picked up speed. "And I don't mean to be a bitch. You just always rub me the wrong way," she added as an afterthought.

"Don't I know it," he mumbled, shaking his head. "Open the door that leads to the bathroom. Ivy left a cloak there she got from who knows where. She said covered in that, you'll be able to walk through the doors with no problem."

"And we trust Ivy so much now…" Artemis snapped but walked towards the door and opening it, looked around. There was a cloak draped over a chair right next to the door, as if Ivy knew Artemis would be reluctant to walk around and search for it.

"Do we have a better option?" Fern asked from behind her.

"No." Grabbing the cloak, she lifted it up to see it better. "I don't suppose we have."

With a deep sigh, Artemis opened the cloak and flung it over her shoulders before pulling the hood over her head. It was pooling down at her feet, covering her completely, and a comforting feeling, almost like an embrace, covered her from head to toe. There was nothing more to say until she'd dealt with Lazarus first, so without delay she grabbed the handle and opened the door.

"Oh, and Artemis?" Fern called out making her lift the hood and look at him over her shoulder. "Kill that fucker and get me out of here. Please!" he pleaded with his eyes as well as his words. Taking a deep breath, she nodded once and walked out of the room.

Chapter Thirty-Nine

Anxiety made Artemis clutch the cloak tightly as she started walking towards the doors. Her mind kept going back to Raphael, but the bond they shared let her know he was still alive. It didn't make the fear for his life disappear, but it was at least comforting to know that he was not gone. She couldn't even entertain that idea at the moment, it was too crippling to even think it as a possibility.

In her human form she couldn't see the red glow around the doors, but as she walked closer and stopped in front of them, she could feel it prickling her skin. Where her face was visible under the hood, it felt like she was standing too close to a blazing fire. Bending her head low to stop the sting, Artemis pushed the cloak towards the intricate door handles, gripping them through the fabric and pushed with all her might.

The massive doors swung open, hitting the walls hard enough that the hollow thud made her chest vibrate. The room was so dark that she couldn't see more than a foot inside it. A horrid stench assaulted her senses and she gagged, swallowing the thick bile that rose up. Parting her lips, she breathed through her mouth as her feet moved silently across the threshold. The urge to shift was overwhelming, but she kept moving forward, straining her ears to hear anything that would tell her where Lazarus was. *If he's even still here,* she thought gloomily.

"Impossible!" The hiss coming from her right made her jump away in the opposite direction, expecting a blow to follow the words.

Artemis couldn't fight her instincts anymore, and since she was already past the warded door, she shifted, ripping the cloak in the process. It fluttered to the ground like a feather. Now she was able to see in the thick darkness, and she coiled up for an attack.

Lazarus was perched on the edge of his bed, holding a glass vial with sparkling liquid inside it. His left wing was hanging limply at the side, like someone had tried to rip it off his back. Pride swelled in her chest knowing that Raphael had managed to do such damage when he attacked. His right wing was slowly mending as she watched, letting her know that whatever it was in that bottle was for healing. He stood frozen, staring at her with wide eyes as if he couldn't believe she was really standing inside his rooms.

Everything her eyes could see was covered in webs and some black sticky goo that was sliding and dropping like chunks of mud. It must be where that horrible smell was coming from, Artemis concluded, before looking back at Lazarus. He had already poured the liquid over his wing and straightened, standing up from the bed.

"I have come to learn that everything is possible nowadays," she told him conversationally as she pulled out one of her arrows. Her glowing eyes reflected off his face as she watched him sneer at her.

"Nothing is possible for you anymore!" With those words, he launched himself in her direction.

Flipping around, she avoided colliding with him, but her legs were moving slower because of all the gunk on the floor. Lazarus crashed with a resounding boom into the wall behind her, making what seemed to be a chest of drawers break into pieces from the impact. Artemis let her wings lift her off the floor as she hovered a foot off the ground. Even with the high ceilings, the rooms weren't large enough for her to move freely. Seeing her chance, she threw the arrow at him with the same speed as if she had used her bow. His roar of pain as it embedded itself in his shoulder was like music to her ears.

Artemis pushed herself towards him while he was reaching behind to rip the arrow out, and she grabbed the hand that was pulling on it. She pulled, too, as his scream echoed everywhere around them. His wings must have healed, so her other hand grabbed the closest one to her and she ripped it from his back with a sickening sucking sound that split the air a second before his scream almost burst her eardrums. She found herself flung back away from him as he flipped her off him like an unwanted shirt. Her body crashed into the bed and the whole frame broke, making Artemis drop to the floor along with it. Still holding onto the massive wing in her hand, she dropped it on the sticky floor and watched, horrified, as it dissolved into the sludge like it was a part of it. Her legs wiggled, trying to find traction so she could lift herself up when Lazarus turned towards her, his face contorted with pain and hatred.

"You stupid fucking fool! We need those damn humans or we will all die here like trash!" Lazarus roared, taking measured steps towards her. "If we have nothing to feed on, we'll all die, you included! You think the whole realm turned gray in a day? You think I'm the worst monster you've seen in your life? Oh, how I pray to be there to see your face the day when you realize I have done everything to assure this realm's safety!"

Artemis kept moving slowly, lifting herself up as she watched him warily. He held her arrow in his fist, and she hoped she'd be able to grab it. It felt wrong to have him touch it, like he was touching her soul. Lazarus saw where her eyes kept flicking and a cruel smile blossomed on his face.

"Just like with your precious weapon, you whore! We are connected to all living things. We feed off their energy to stay alive. We cannot feed off our own, so we destroyed this realm. If that portal doesn't open, we're all doomed!"

"And you didn't think of that before you killed my mother and made the humans close the portal?" Artemis snapped at him while she felt sick, thinking about the idea of feeding off living beings.

It wasn't like it was any different from what the vampires did, but it sure sounded wrong. With the Fae, they were unaware that their life was being consumed with each second. No wonder the humans made sure the portal closed. *Was that what I was doing while walking around in their world?* The thought floated in her head, but she pushed it away.

"I didn't do anything but take what I was entitled to! We are the top of the food chain. Humans are there to please us. They do it willingly!"

"I'm sure they willingly die!" She told him dryly as she finally stood up. "Just like you will die willingly now!"

Lazarus was so preoccupied in his speech about humans

that he didn't expect her to throw herself at him or to have pulled out two more arrows from behind her. As they collided face to face, she watched his eyes widen in surprise as she felt the arrows sink through his skin and embed themselves so deep it would take her several tries to pull them out. She hugged him, holding him close as her smile grew. The shocked expression on his face was the best gift he could've given her. The green glow from his eyes started fading as the air wheezed from his lips.

"You fool!" he whispered. "I gave my soul to keep the real monsters at bay. Look around you! This was the price I paid to keep our home safe from the demons that were trying to connect a portal to our realm. The cave will open now…All of you will die when no one can hold the back portal closed!"

She frowned at him, but his lashes fluttered and closed as he went limp in her arms. Angrily she dropped him on the floor and bent down to take hold of the arrows. Pulling a few times, she dislodged them from his chest and looked around. A chill filled the air, and she walked out of the room without even thinking of the wards. Luckily, they must have dissolved with his death. Stopping just outside the doors, Artemis looked back over her shoulder. This should've been a happy moment, when she finally found her mother's killer. Lazarus was no longer in the room. His body had vanished and she remembered the way his wing dissolved in the gunk, making her shiver with dread. Instead of a moment to celebrate a victory, why did it feel like it was just the beginning of a horrible nightmare?

Chapter Forty

It took two days for Ivy to heal Raphael and another two days for Artemis to feed him her blood and take care of him until he was finally allowed to get out of bed. Fern disappeared sometime between the death of Lazarus and Artemis bringing Raphael to Ivy's room. The Fae that sided with Lazarus scattered throughout the realm, licking their wounds, while the rest took up residence within the palace walls. Patrols were sent out daily to check the perimeter for anything out of the ordinary.

Artemis didn't care much about what Lazarus said before he died until Ivy confirmed that something more sinister then him was lurking in the shadows. For centuries she had been looking forward to the moment when her mother's killer would die by her hand, but Artemis didn't feel the closure that she expected. So many things were left hanging in the air, many unknown things still lurked, waiting to bite them when they least expected it.

She watched Raphael's face as he slept. His long lashes cast shadows on his cheekbones as they fluttered gently while he dreamed. His eyes moved restlessly under the closed eyelids, and she pressed her lips gently on them. Ever since the fight with Lazarus, he kept waking at odd times to watchher sleep or pulling her tightly to his chest and holding her like someone was trying to take her away. It warmed her heart to feel the love he had for her, not just through their bond but through his actions as well. The light knocks on the door made him snap his eyes open and grab for her to cover her with his body. Artemis smiled at him as she cupped his face.

"It's probably Ivy, Raphael." Artemis waited until his green eyes focused on her face. "She's the only one coming here to check on you since you almost decapitated the guard that was bringing food." She chuckled softly, making his lips twitch at the corners.

"You were naked," he mumbled, looking at her beautiful face with her violet hair spread around her head like a cloud while her eyes glowed slightly like jewels. His eyes dropped to her full lips. "I don't like anyone else seeing you naked!"

"Yes, you still hold onto a barbaric human trait," she drawled "We made sure everyone in the palace knows." She grinned at him as he opened his mouth to say something but the knocking started again.

"Go away!" Raphael growled loud enough that the knocking stopped.

He was bending his head down to capture Artemis's tempting lips in a kiss when the door flew open and banged off the opposite wall. Raphael pushed himself up, flipping around in midair and bared his fangs at whoever was stupid enough to enter. Ivy stood at the door with her arms crossed over her chest, glaring at him as her golden glow sparkled as if agitated. She almost looked like a mother frustrated with her disobedient child. It made Artemis press a hand to her mouth to keep from laughing out loud at both of them. A snort escaped, and Raphael turned his head to glare at her. Unable to stop herself, Artemis laughed.

"Don't be angry with me, I'm just an observer," she chuckled and lifted her arms in surrender as his glower deepened.

"He can be angry some other time!" Ivy snapped "We have a problem!"

"What kind of problem?" Artemis jumped off the bed, all laughter gone.

"The portal room started glowing not long ago, but nothing's coming through." A frown pulled Ivy's eyebrows down, wrinkling her forehead. It looked strange to see her like that, but urgency spurred them on when she mumbled, "It's still not time!"

"Let's see what's going on." Raphael didn't wait to hear what else she had to say and pushed his way past her, wearing only loose sleep pants sitting low on his hips while he was bare-chested. The muscles on his broad back kept Artemis mesmerized as they bunched and jumped with each movement he made and she stood there for a second before snapping herself out of it. Artemis hurried after him with Ivy following them both.

As they neared the portal rooms, Artemis and Raphael stopped in their tracks, almost causing Ivy to collide with them both. Voices were coming from there, and as they heard it, they looked at each other. Raphael's eyebrows nearly hit his hairline, but Artemis couldn't help but smile.

"Get your stupid hands off me, you ape! I don't care who you are, I will fry your ass!" Iris snapped over her shoulder as she ran out of the room, trying to dodge the grabbing hands. She bounced off Raphael's chest and with a loud 'oomph' dropped on her ass at his feet, her long hair covering her face before she flipped it over her head hurriedly.

"Get back here, human!" The guard came rushing out and stopped dead in his tracks at seeing Artemis, his yellow eyes flashing in panic in his porcelain face. "I tried to stop her, but she's slippery as a snake!" He glared at Iris and pointed at her accusingly.

"It's fine. She means no harm," Artemis told him as guilt hit her full force. In her fear for Raphael, she forgot all about Iris. "I'm sorry, Iris, I never thought you'd be able to walk through the portal or I would've told the guards to watch for you." She offered her hand and pulled Iris to her feet.

"Yeah," Dusting her pants, even though the floors were so clean they could be used as mirrors, Iris glared at Artemis and Raphael. "Neither did I, until I had no other choice!"

"What happened?" Raphael looked her up and down searching for injuries. "You don't look harmed."

"Don't listen to him, he's grumpy." Artemis smacked him lightly on his bare chest with the back of her hand. "Tell us what's wrong."

"Your buddy Claude lied!" Iris snarled at Raphael, making confusion cloud his face. "He remembers everything! And he has friends! I'm lucky I managed to open the portal, thanks to this." Pulling the arrow from her jacket, she waved it in their face until Artemis took it gently from her fingers. "He was going to kill me. I had no other choice!" Iris looked desperately from one to the other. "I don't know where Fern went. Luckily he woke up, not five minutes before we heard them coming through the front door of the shop. So we ran, but we had to split up. I just hope he finds the portal soon. There were so many of them!"

"Calm down, no one will harm you here." Artemis gripped her shoulders, making Iris nod as she gulped air to calm herself down. Artemis remembered what Lazarus had said about Fae feeding off human life and dropped her hands to her sides. Praying that she told the truth, she looked at Iris. "We will find Fern and we will deal with Claude."

Iris stopped panting, and Artemis almost smiled until she realized that that Iris wasn't even breathing. The witch was holding her breath while looking over her shoulder with green eyes as round as dinner plates. Before Artemis could ask what was wrong, Iris blinked, sucking up a deep breath.

"It's you!" she whispered as she lifted a shaky finger.

Looking over her shoulder, Artemis saw Ivy smiling wickedly at Iris. There was a sparkle in her eyes as she watched the witch.

"Yes, It's me!" Ivy's musical voice rang around them. "And finally the ancient line is here so we can find the first secret! A little early from what I thought the timeline would be, which is surprising, but there might be hope for us after all!" She beamed at everyone.

Artemis and Raphael groaned at the same time as Iris looked around confused.

"I had a feeling this wasn't over just yet!" Raphael rubbed both his hands over his face.

"Oh, don't be a spoilsport now, Raphael. Think of all the fun we're going to have hunting!" A wicked smile lifted the corners of Artemis's lips as her violet eyes bore in the green panicked ones of Iris.

"I should've just let that asshole kill me, I think." Iris groaned as Ivy's musical laughter rang around the halls.

Next in the Hidden Portals Trilogy Series

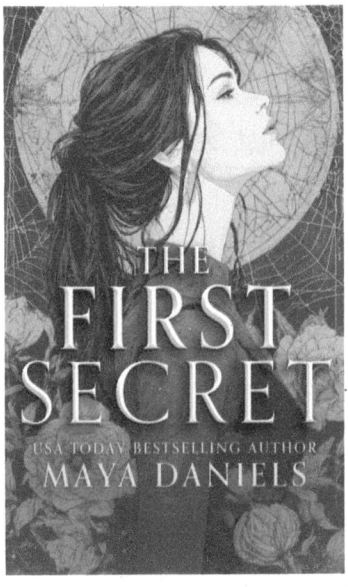

vinci-books.com/firstsecret

Can love survive when everything you know is a lie?

Iris, a solitary witch, finds her peaceful life shattered by visions that challenge her self-perception. Fern, a Fae desperate to save his dying people, is drawn to protect Iris, even if it means following her into the depths of hell. As they onfront the dark forces that threaten both their worlds, an undeniable attraction blooms between them. Can Iris and Fern overcome the odds stacked against them, or will the truth of their origins tear them apart?

Turn the page for a free preview…

The First Secret: Prologue

Sitting cross-legged in the middle of the large room dedicated to her goddess, clutching the Fae arrow in her trembling hands, Iris stared at nothing. The last remnants of the portal she'd opened for Artemis and Raphael were fading. Little flashes of sparks reminded her of her situation. Iris kept the portal open for a long time, unsure if she was hallucinating. Without thought her thumb stroked the arrow. Zaps of magic shot up her arm numbing it all the way to the shoulder. Her magic spread around the room like a curious sentient entity in the form of tendrils of dark purple smoke.

Iris didn't register the candles floating in midair all around her, their flames flaring in bursts as the markings on the arrow glowed with a blueish spark. Part of her brain knew that she should release it and prepare to pull the stubborn vampire out of the Fae realm, yet, she sat there.

'Never make a deal with the devil on an empty stomach' her mother used to say, but Iris had never understood the meaning of it until a week ago. Curiosity had always got her into trouble. She'd never learned the lesson to stay out of things that didn't concern her, and surviving her current peculiar predicament seemed unlikely.

At first, that damn vampire had intrigued her with his beauty. Not handsome, that would've meant he possessed some imperfection that made him at least a little human. Iris didn't see any harm in letting him watch her ritual. In her defense, no sane woman would've said no to Raphael hanging around. So, stupidly, she'd helped him when he brought Artemis to her, unconscious and hardly breathing. Iris realized that the vampire would never look at any other woman but the one he cradling to his chest like the most precious thing in the world. Being honest with herself, she knew that she only tried to like Raphael because she couldn't get a certain man out of her head. Well a Fae, not a man, but that made no difference to her stupid heart.

A prickling sensation, like fire ants crawling all over her body, jolted her out of her internal musings. She couldn't remember the last time she'd been this jumpy but having crazy immortals around, itching for a fight, would do that to a person. Another wave hit her as she tried to push herself up off the floor. Stumbling and nearly falling on her face, Iris hurried, holding the hem of her dress in both hands but not letting go of the arrow. She'd promised Artemis that she would be ready if they needed her, and she'd be damned if she didn't keep her word. The arrow would be glued to her until everything settled.

The prickling intensified as she jerked the heavy door open and ran down the hall. Only someone trying to break through one of her protections could cause this internal burning. She'd placed one around the store after the fiasco with the vampire king. Otherwise, there was only one thing she protected here, and no one but her knew about that.

With her heart in her throat, she ran through the curtain separating the store from the rooms behind it, and almost tripped over her feet in the process.

"Damn curtains and stupid hallways..." she muttered while flailing her arms to detangle herself from the black fabric. Bursting into the store she almost toppled a couple of statues to the floor.

The few LAD candles with their fake flames gave off only enough light to make out objects. Still, not wanting to break anything, she tiptoed carefully towards the large front windows. The streetlight provided enough yellowish hue that even before reaching the glass Iris could tell no one lurked there. The feeling of her insides burning increased, and her eyebrows scrunched up in confusion and pain when nothing but an occasional vehicle passed by.

The arrow in her hand hummed proving that either Artemis, or Raphael, was in trouble, yet the urge to find out who was trying to get through her protection grew stronger. Reaching for the doorknob in hopes of finding answers outside the store, she jumped when something topped over in the hallway and a voice muttered.

Panic gripped her like an iron fist, Iris Forgot about vamps, Fae and their realm. Her feet barely touched the ground as she ran to the back rooms. At the end of the hallway, in front of an empty wall, a figure hunched over picking up a fallen painting.

"Danny?" Gasping for air, Iris bent over. Placing her hands on her knees, she almost nicked herself with the arrow.

With a high-pitched shriek, the blond woman dropped on her ass, her eyes as wide as dinner plates as she clutched her chest with both hands.

"Oh my god, Iris! You scared the crap out of me!"

"Your god is not here, Danny, and I'll scare even more crap out of you if you don't tell me what you are doing here." Still gasping, Iris glared at the other woman.

"I work here." Danny lifted her eyebrows clearly wondering if her boss had lost her mind. "Remember?"

"I didn't mean in the store, smartass. I meant here, in the hallway."

"Oh..." Danny fidgeted with her hands before slowly lifting herself up without looking at Iris. "I had an urge to check this area." Her face turned red, and she stumbled over her words. "You always talk about intuition, and just knowing stuff, and I had this thing." She gazed shyly at Iris. "Like a knowing... that I needed to come here. But then I bumped the painting, and then you scared the crap out of me... To be honest, I thought Raphael was here." Danny's face turned beet red, as she looked at anything but Iris.

"Go home, Danny." Iris pressed a hand over her forehead. "Forget about the vampire, he is nothing but trouble. Take a few days off, and I'll see you next week. I need some time to sort things out."

"Am I getting fired?" Danny's chin trembled.

"Why on earth would you think that? No, I just think after everything, we could both use a break."

"That's true." With a relieved sigh, Danny smiled tightly, and without another word walked towards the store front.

Iris stood there, heart thundering, thanking whoever watched over her for hiding her panic at Danny's intuition calling her to this very spot. As soon as the blonde hair disappeared through the curtain, Iris turned and traced an invisible line on the wall from top to bottom with her hand. Not touching it, her fingers hovered an inch or so from the plaster. The purple glow emitted from her palm reflected on the wall, lighting it up and revealing the door that no one else but her could detect. It troubled her that Danny would stop at this very spot. Swallowing the nervousness, Iris pushed the door open and stepped inside.

It was a small room, a 'just in case' hideaway. Nothing in it apart from a bed, a chair and a dresser with a few medical supplies, some clothing, and blankets. Everything looked identical to how she'd left it, including the sleeping Fae who had not woken since the day he'd been pulled into this realm alongside Artemis via a portal during one of her rituals. The same Fae who had haunted her thoughts ever since. He resembled a sculpture rather than a living being. His long silky black hair spread out around his unusually perfect face and his pointy ears peeked out of it. Unable to help herself, Iris reached out and traced his angular jaw and full lips with her fingers. She'd been willing him to wake up for over a week, but nothing helped. As she'd done every day since he'd arrived, she prepared to send her magic inside him, to make sure he still lived.

A terrified scream echoed around the store and hallway. Iris's head snapped toward the closed door and the blood drained from her face. Danny's voice echoed in a painful scream a moment before sounds of breaking glass and the stock being smashed and turned over. Her mind stuttered trying to think of what to do. Terror paralyzed her when a voice she recognized echoed out from the store.

"Witch! You better show yourself, or your little friend here will give more than just a little blood," Claude called out.

"Shit! Crappity crap...damn it!" Iris muttered through clenched teeth knowing she had nowhere to run. More crashing came from the shop before energy stirred in the hallway as Claude passed the curtain.

"Witch, witch, witch…" He sang the word in some mocking song as he banged his fist on the walls. "Come out, come out, witch."

Taking a deep breath, Iris squared her shoulders. Claude might possess more physical strength, he'd almost killed her once, but she wasn't a helpless little puppy. She had teeth, and she would bite if cornered. And she was cornered, if she wanted to protect the unconscious Fae from the vampire. Steeling herself, she gripped the arrow tighter in her fist and stepped towards the door. Her heart froze, and her feet gave out when a thick arm wrapped around her waist and another grabbed her mouth cutting off her automatic scream. A second later, the scent of rainforest and freshly cut grass filled her nostrils making her sag in the hold of the man behind her.

"Don't make a sound, witch. We need to run," Fern whispered from behind her, his deep musical voice making her shiver. "We need to run, now!"

The First Secret: Chapter One

"Oh, hell no!" With her eyebrows pulled down, and her hands on her hips, Iris glared at Raphael and Artemis. "I'm not going anywhere with that lying weirdo, and there is nothing you can say to convince me otherwise!" Stomping her foot for emphasis, and angrily pointing a finger at Ivy, she lifted her chin.

"Witch, you're pushing your luck right now, and patience is not one of my strong suits," Raphael growled through clenched teeth.

"It's not?" Iris gasped pressing her hands on her chest. "I never would've guessed!" She did everything she could to maintain her innocent expression although Artemis snickering didn't help.

"You are encouraging her obnoxious behavior." Raphael turned his disapproving glare on his mate. Artemis raised one eyebrow. That's all it took for the stubborn vampire to turn to mush and give her a soft smile.

"You have no right in this realm, or the next, to call anyone obnoxious, especially after what I witnessed!" Not deterred, Iris continued by waving a finger in the vampire's face.

His gaze narrowed. Lightning fast, he snatched her finger in his large hand. Iris didn't expect it, and pure instinct made her magic light up like a Christmas tree in her chest. It burst out of her and knocked him a few feet in the air before he dropped into a cat-like crouch. Eyes glowing and fangs bared, Raphael appeared almost feral. Iris lifted both hands to protect herself in case he pounced. Artemis moved in front of her to calm Raphael down, but Ivy stood to the side watching everything unfold with a huge smile on her face. It pissed Iris off even more.

"Raphael." Even Iris shivered at Artemis's low sultry tone. "She is scared and worried. Her life was in danger because of us, because of me, and we were not there to protect her as we promised. Lashing out at you is her way of dealing with it."

"I'm neither scared, not worried just so we are clear," Iris chirped from behind Artemis making Ivy chuckle.

"You're not helping." Looking over her shoulder, Artemis looked pointedly at Ivy.

"Okay, fine!" Huffing, Iris crossed her arms over her chest. "Sorry boss man, I didn't mean to zap you. In my defense, you startled me. And ever since I stepped foot here, my magic has been flaring up. I'm trying my best to keep it under control." She shrugged, but no one was fooled at her nonchalance. Her expressive green eyes betrayed the fear lurking inside.

They were standing outside the palace where Artemis had taken Iris to show her the extent of the deterioration of the realm. The Dreamweaver, Ivy, was adamant that Iris was of the ancient line needed to heal the realm of the Fae. Iris wanted to argue about that little detail, she figured it'd be useless. Every time she tried to explain that she didn't understand where her magic came from, Ivy cut her mid-sentence, saying that time would prove it.

The hairs on the back of Iris's neck prickled and she scanned the area without being obvious about it. Someone was watching her, and anxiety swirled in her stomach.

"You are a walking disaster, witch." Raphael, ignorant of her unease, continued. "Maybe it would be smarter to send you back to the human realm." Blood drained from Iris's face. "I'm worried the Fae might kill you if one of us is not around you." Placing his hands on his hips, he looked at her solemnly as if he'd stated the most reasonable solution to her problems.

"No…" her voice was barely above a whisper as she forced that one word through numb lips.

"You don't know what you are talking about, bloodsucker!" Ivy's face darkened, dimming the golden glow around her. "Are you trying to doom us all by getting her killed?"

"She can't control her magic! Any of the warriors would skin her alive if she did that to them! She doesn't think, she reacts!"

"Now listen to me, and listen very good, you bullheaded man!" Ivy snarled, not caring that Artemis gave her a side-eye while Raphael glared.

Iris missed the rest of the exchange as Artemis threaded her arm through hers and pulled her towards the large open double doors of the palace. Iris let Artemis lead her. Her mind still spun from the creepy sensation of being watched, plus Raphael's comment about sending her back to where Claude waited. The Fae milling around the front courtyard stopped and bowed their heads in respect, placing their fists over their heart as they had done ever since Artemis killed Lazarus. Iris ignored them.

"I don't want to go inside the palace," she blurted. Artemis stopped in her tracks and raised her eyebrows.

"Don't ask for a reason right now, I can't give you one. I just feel like I'll never come out alive if I walk through those doors." Iris was grateful that Artemis didn't dismiss her like Raphael would've done.

Artemis might be a ruthless bitch, feared by Fae and vampires alike, but the other woman never did anything simply for the sake of hurting or killing someone. Iris felt a kinship connecting them, and at the moment her only hope to stay alive lay in Artemis's hands.

"Talk to me, Iris." Looking at her intently, Artemis grabbed her shoulders. "You know you can tell me anything. Who has scared you so much under my roof?"

"No one, I swear." Shaking her head in frustration, Iris sighed deeply. "I can't explain it... There is someone...no, there is something inside watching me. I can feel it every time I'm inside the palace, and I also felt it when we were standing outside."

"I'm not dismissing your worries, my friend. But, I'm not sure if you have noticed, my kind kinda likes you." With her lips curling up in a smile, Artemis tilted her chin indicating the Fae walking around them. "We like pretty things," she winked at Iris, "and you are a beautiful woman. Plus, not many of them have seen the human realm. To us, you are exotic, unusual. If you need to let off some steam, I'm sure many will be more than happy to take on the task. From what I know, humans don't have a problem with casual sex."

"Oh my god, no!" Iris looked at her friend, horrified. "Some humans don't have a problem with it, but most do. I'm one of those. The ones that mind." Waving her hand as if chasing a fly, Iris sighed again. "This is different from being checked out. I'm sure I look like a circus monkey to them and that's why they're staring. I mean, look at them!" Moving her arm in an arc, she indicated all the drool-worthy specimens around her. "They are so perfect, they don't look real... or normal. Me? I'm just, I donno... human?" Chuckling humorlessly, she covered her face with her hands. "I sound pathetic and like a scared little mouse. It's so not me; I have no idea why I'm acting like this."

Artemis's jaw clenched. "Raphael!" called to her mate so loudly that Iris jumped a little.

"What's wrong?" Before the echo of Artemis's voice faded Raphael was next to them fangs gleaming and eyes glowing. Iris stared with her eyebrows up to her hairline, as confused at Artemis's reaction as Raphael seemed.

"Search the palace." Not taking her gaze off Iris, Artemis pursed her lips and released a soft whistle that had dozens of warriors almost materialize around them with hands on their weapons. "Search with all your senses, not only your sight. We have an uninvited guest that I want to personally welcome to our realm. I want to see whoever it is alive and on their knees in front of me by tonight."

Grab your copy...
vinci-books.com/firstsecret

About the Author

Maya Daniels, USA Today Bestselling and multi-award-winning supernatural suspense author, is a fun-loving woman with many talents.

She traveled the world, gaining life experiences that helped her career as an investigative journalist, as well as her storytelling. Maya writes compelling tales of magic, mythical creatures, loyalty, and life-changing friendships with snarky female characters—much like herself.

Her travels have taken her to Europe, Africa, Asia, Australia, and America. Born with her feet in motion, she currently resides in Ohio, spinning her next epic story that you will not want to put down.

Her biggest 'sins' are her love of chocolate and coffee—through an IV drip! One to never sit still, Maya practices Reiki healing, different types of martial arts, reads about the arcane, talks to furry creatures more than humans, picks up a sledgehammer for home improvement, and travels with her fated mate, seeking her own adventures.

www.ingramcontent.com/pod-product-compliance
Ingram Content Group UK Ltd.
Pitfield, Milton Keynes, MK11 3LW, UK
UKHW040252230426
470297UK00004B/104

9 781036 705893